# MURDER IN THE LIBRARY

WEATHERBORO MYSTERIES BOOK 1

CP FRAISE

Copyright © 2020 by CP FRAISE

All rights reserved.

Cover Design by CP Fraise

Cover picture and Chapter Headers purchased from istockphoto.com

First Edition October 2020

All rights reserved. No part of this book may be reproduced, distributed, or transmitted, in any form or by any means, electronic or mechanical, including photocopying, recording, or any information storage and retrieval systems, without written permission from the author, except for the use of brief quotations in a book review or permitted by law.

This book is a work of fiction. Names, characters, places and incidents are the product of the author's imagination. Any resemblance to any actual person, living or dead, events or locales is entirely coincidental. All trademarks are owned by the relevant companies and are used for reference purposes in this book only.

Ebook ISBN: 978-1-8382197-0-3

Paperback ISBN: 978-1-8382197-1-0

 Created with Vellum

*For the people who encouraged me when writing this book. It was tough but you kept me going.*
*Thank you,*

# CONTENTS

# 1

THIBAULT

**October 2017**

My life had gone through so many changes in the past four months. After unexpectedly inheriting a house from a great-aunt I never met, I moved to the town of Weatherboro. I'd wanted to come live closer to my parents in Charleston, and this was serendipity. Plus, I had landed a position at the local library.

So far, I was really enjoying my job. Being surrounded by books and people who loved them as much as I did was wonderful. I was slowly developing friendships with people I'd met at the café Miracle Brew like George and Sam. Being sociable came from my French mother and was one of the traits I was most thankful for from that heritage.

Going to the Miracle Brew at least twice a week for coffee, a treat, and fresh gossip had become a routine. This morning I ordered drinks and treats for myself and my coworkers. Having served them on more than one occasion while working here, I knew their preferences. I moved away from the counter without really looking and ran smack-dab into a powerful chest. Already uttering an apology, I tried to move back when I slipped on something and started falling backward. Two muscular arms stopped my descent.

Looking into emerald green eyes, I couldn't utter a word. A gargled sound escaped me. What a brilliant first impression. He smiled, but somehow it quickly turned into a scowl.

Sam, leaning over the counter, shouted, "Thibault. Are you alright?"

I looked at Sam, then my rescuer, then Sam again. I heard a giggle and noticed George grinning at me.

"Found another victim, Thibault?"

My rescuer took a step back, righting me in the process. I tried clearing my throat. The scowl on the man's face deepened.

Both Sam and George turned to him, and George explained. "Hey, Jack. This is Thibault Abrams. He just moved here a month ago or so in Ruth's place and is our new librarian. Thibault, this is Jack Tomlins. One of the detectives at the precinct. You've met Marcus, and this is his partner."

"Aren't there, like, only two detectives?" I remarked. Of all the things to say. Not sorry or thanks, but trivial questions were no problem? Thank you, brain.

"Yes, that's correct," Jack replied in a gruff voice.

Oh boy, didn't his tone shoot straight to my dick.

I smiled at him, then tried to talk. In retrospect, I should have kept my mouth shut and bowed. It would have been less embarrassing. "I. Um. Thank you, sir. I mean, Jack. I mean, officer. Um. Clumsy seems to be my middle name. It's nice to meet you. I don't think I met you before. And god only knows I would remember a man like you. Not that there is anything wrong with you. To the contrary. I mean..." I waved my hand, encompassing his entire body, as if what I was saying wasn't clear or embarrassing enough. "Anyway, what brings you here? I mean, other than coffee." I let out the weirdest laugh of my life. High-pitched and snorty. My donkey brayed more nicely than this.

All three men stared at me like I had grown a third eye. Sam and George seemed horrified and amused, and Jack's scowl deepened.

One of Sam's employees saved me, calling my name as my order was ready. I rushed to the counter, grabbed my drinks, and ran out the door, barely shouting a goodbye over my shoulder. Which made me almost run into someone else. This was so mortifying. And both my friends would get an earful later. Thank you for the rescue. Not.

Today we were having a little council of war at work. The city was growing and the budget was slowly trickling back in. Still, the mayor's office was considering shutting down the library, as it didn't bring in any revenue and attendance had dropped in recent years.

The meeting was lively, full of great ideas. I was scared this would all backfire, but we didn't really have a choice.

**Nine Months Later - June 2018**

I was so done. On top of the heat, thunderstorms, and people's tempers flaring, I had walked into the library three days ago to find out we'd had a break-in.

Hadn't that been fun? Detective Joyful and Marcus came over to investigate. The heat made Detective Tomlins even grumpier than usual, which was saying something.

From there, things only got worse. We had needed cleaners to come in and we'd had to do a small fundraiser to pay for minor repairs and the cleaning costs, as the mayor's office turned down our request for help. The mayor was currently campaigning to be reelected and definitely wouldn't have my vote. Too busy squandering our money on failed projects instead of investing in the community and his public servants.

We were laughed out of the city council for requesting a small camera be installed at our back entrance, just in case. After consulting with a lawyer, they said we could privately invest in one. So we all chipped in, and after multiple YouTube tutorials, we installed it on a streetlamp opposite our side entrance.

We weren't the only ones affected. A slew of robberies occurred around town. At least we were lucky. They hadn't damaged anything of value or stolen anything apart from petty cash. Some other businesses weren't so lucky. Neither was my friend George, as one of his antique typewriters was stolen. He had a few in his collection, but this was one of his most valuable.

Right when I was about to leave work, my phone rang.

Seeing Sam's name, I quickly answered, "Hey, Sammy. How is it going?"

"Hey, sweetie. I am good. Hope you are too. Tell me— who has his bag in his car and is on his way to my place so we can have drinks, a good night's sleep, and then go partyyy?"

I laughed. "I don't know. Why don't you enlighten me?"

His screech was so loud, I had to move the phone away from my ear. He shouted, "Are you kidding me? Don't tell me you forgot. I know there is a lot going on at the moment, but please, please tell me you didn't forget. Hell, that's the one thing one can never forget!"

"Ok, drama queen, cool your jets. I know. Don't worry. I

was about to close. I wouldn't miss it for the world, you know it. I can't wait for tomorrow night."

Sam laughed in my ear. "Come on, stop talking and hurry over so we can get started."

The next night found us in Charleston, where we enjoyed one exciting and memorable night. Or at least I did. I didn't know it would change my life in the years to come quite the way it did.

❧

## Jack

I was pleased to see the end of the workday. Our shift was uneventful. Apart from the robberies, neither Marcus or I, had much to do. We helped some of the officers on a nasty call for a domestic disturbance, but that was it. The precinct was all abuzz with the mayor's election going on at the moment. At the station, we all wondered who would replace our current chief. He was retiring, and we knew change was coming.

I pushed the thoughts away as I made my way home. Today was Pride, and though the planning had been left in the hands of Marcus, my best friend and partner on the force, I was looking forward to the promise of some alcohol and cele-brating.

Freshly showered and ready to go, I went to Marcus's place. When he opened the door, I knew ignorance wasn't bliss.

He was wearing white-and-gold clothes with an intricate golden mask contrasting beautifully with his dark skin. Behind it, his brown eyes were sparkling at me.

"What the hell, Marcus?" Another head popped over his shoulder, wearing a mask as well. The white and blue went well with his tan skin and inky hair. What I could see of his outfit was blue too. There was only one other man Marcus could always rope into any of his schemes—our friend Bobby.

They both looked at me with matching grins, then both shouted "Ta-da" while doing jazz hands. I wished I could say this was brought on by an excess of alcohol, but I knew it definitely wasn't the case. I loved these two men dearly, but sometimes they scared me. I was the quiet one of the group. Keeping up with them had often given me palpitations growing up, and even more so now.

"I see. Goodnight then, gentlemen." Before I could turn around and make my escape, they both pulled me inside. I wasn't a small man by any means and was taller than both of them, but they worked out, often together, and were a lot stronger than they looked. And they looked plenty strong as it was.

They sat me down on the couch, both taking a seat on Marcus's coffee table, which creaked in protest. Poor thing.

"Jack. My man. Your outfit is in my bathroom waiting just for you." Seeing I was about to speak, he raised a hand and continued. "Don't. I know what you will say. Don't worry, we are not staying here. We are going to a hotel in Charleston. We got lucky. They had a last-minute cancellation. Yes, you can still take your car in case you decide it's too much for you. Now go get changed."

I was about to ask why we had to be in costume to go anywhere when they yanked me out of my seat and propelled me toward the bathroom.

On one hand, I knew if I said no, they would respect it and go without me. On the other hand, I really needed to let out some steam, and this wasn't the weirdest, craziest, or most revealing costume Marcus had made me wear over the years. I decided to go with the flow. I could always say no once I changed if it really was too far out of my comfort zone.

While I put on the tight black T-shirt and skintight black jeans, the other two talked and giggled in the sitting room. We always seemed to revert to our teenage selves when we got together. It could last a few minutes or the entire time we hung out.

Once changed, I put on the intricate and sexy black lace mask and surveyed the effect in the mirror. My black lace jockstrap made me feel even sexier and naughtier.

I rejoined the guys in the sitting room. "You were right. I don't hate it."

"And your ass looks hot in those jeans," said Bobby. I loved how the only straight man in the room was often the one confident enough to hand us compliments on our looks. He told us once that if women could do it all the time to their friends, then why couldn't he?

Marcus smirked. "I know. I chose those on purpose. I made him buy them a long time ago, and he never wears them. I thought it was the occasion."

I didn't question how he got ahold of my clothes. We were at each other's houses often enough; I wouldn't have noticed him taking them.

"All right. What's the plan?" I asked.

"Like I said before, we go to Charleston and go from there."

"That's it?"

"There is a masquerade type of party at the Booty Shaker. It doesn't start until at least ten p.m., so we can go for food and drinks beforehand."

"Sounds good to me."

Bobby stood, all excited puppy, and shouted, "Let's go party."

Bobby and Marcus drove away in one car, and I took mine.

I might stay with them for the night, but I knew myself. I wasn't a big fan of clubs or dancing, and whether or not I hooked up with someone, I grew bored pretty fast with those kinds of settings.

Once there, we had a great time. The food was good, and we drank for a while, though I stopped earlier than the other two. We went to the Booty Shaker shortly after ten thirty. The place was already packed. Once we had drinks—water for me, beers and shots for them—they left me to go dance while I watched from where I stood. The dance floor was a sea of bodies, all weaving together on whatever song was playing. The heavy beats made my heart thump in my chest.

I wasn't a big fan of dancing, but I did like crowd watching. Especially when the view was men clad in very little, all shapes and sizes rubbing against each other. It was hot, both the atmosphere and the scene in front of me. Bobby and Marcus danced with each other, attracting quite a bit of attention. That usually worked in Marcus's favor. Bobby was good at letting people down gently.

My gaze kept drifting back to the left, where I spotted a mesmerizing man. The way he moved to the rhythm was beautiful to watch. I could mostly see his back and parts of his profile. He wore short shorts and a dark blue fishnet shirt topped with a shoulder harness. His long dark hair was draped over one shoulder, leaving the other one exposed and revealing a gorgeous neck.

He only seemed to dance with two women, laughing and shouting at each other over the music. Every time a man, whether big or small, tried to insert himself between them or dance behind him, he kept shaking his head. A couple other men danced close to him who would intervene, then go back to dancing with each other. Clearly, they were all together, but two wanted to play and this one did not.

During one upbeat song, they all moved around and he turned, staring straight at me. His half-lidded eyes bore into mine, and I couldn't look away. His face, or what I could see of it through the shadows, was stunning. Something was familiar about him, but I couldn't place it. When one of his friends grabbed his attention, the spell was broken. I turned to the bar and ordered another glass of water. After downing it in one go, I made my way down a long corridor to the bathroom.

To get there, I went past a dark room. The sounds and smells told me exactly the type of things going on in there. Along the way were alcoves and nooks, some with curtains, others without, and people were engaged in various acts. This was not going to help me in the bathroom, as my dick definitely took notice of what was happening around me.

I did my thing and headed back to the dance floor. I'd had enough and was ready to go home. Before I reached the end of the corridor, a hand grabbed me and pulled me into one of the alcoves. I turned, ready to give whoever it was a piece of my mind, thinking it was going to be a tall guy. I was not a small man, and moving me took effort.

When I looked at him, I realized two things. For one, this man was much shorter than I'd expected. And second, his outfit was a dark blue fishnet top, booty shorts, and a harness —the man I had been staring at all night. He must have liked what he'd seen and took my walk to the bathroom as an invitation, I guessed.

Being so close to him felt electric. He leaned closer to me and whispered, "Hey, big guy. Fancy meeting you here. Wanna steal time with me?" Something about his voice reminded me of someone as well, but I couldn't place it. He had a slight accent, nothing too noticeable, but I heard it. Compared to the dance floor, the corridor was quiet, though the thump of the bass still made my heart beat hard in my chest. Or it could have been this man's breath on my cheek and his hand still holding my arm.

In the semidarkness, his features were hidden in contrast and shadows. The impression of familiarity increased tenfold. He looked so much like the one man I kept avoiding back in town—Thibault Abrams. Sexy as hell with a tendency for clumsiness and pushing all of my buttons. Something about him rubbed me the wrong way, almost from the beginning. The attraction I felt for him, his sassiness, and how he'd come to town only because a woman I loved like a grandmother had passed away made me resent him.

Why I decided this sexy man was him was one twisted thing I didn't want to examine too closely.

After a few seconds, I realized my not answering was making him reconsider and feel self-conscious, so I did the only thing I could think of: I bent down to kiss him. With my size and build, people expected me to be this big plundering Viking, but I wasn't. I hated hookups because I wanted someone to take control and guide me. Men, especially smaller ones, wanted me to lead, whether because they thought I expected it of them or because they really loved it, I would never know.

To see if I was finally lucky and had found the guy who would take charge, I always opened with a soft kiss. If they pulled back and asked for more, then I knew it would be a pleasant experience but not what I really wanted. Only twice had a man taken control. It hadn't worked out, as they weren't interested in anything long term, but I kept looking.

I bent down fast and then, at the last second, pressed my lips ever so gently against his. At first, neither of us moved further. But the heat coursing through my veins made me want to deepen the kiss, experiment be damned. Something about it ignited my insides in ways no one ever did. Just as I was about to kiss him harder, he lifted on his toes, grabbed my hair roughly, and pressed me against the wall, his tongue seeking entrance. On a sigh, I happily granted it. He was forceful and gentle all at once, biting on my lower lip while moving back to peer at me. Whatever he saw there made him smile.

He nibbled at my jaw on his way to my ear and whispered, "Want to show me what a good boy you can be?" That voice, combined with the smell of lavender and pine invading my nose, made me almost jerk back. I was not dreaming—this was Thibault. He pulled my head back further, making me arch into him, rubbing his hardness against mine, biting gently at my neck. God, he was everything I had ever looked for. Instead of answering, I slowly let myself go down to my knees, giving him plenty of time to stop me.

Once there, I simply gazed at him and waited. He caressed my hair and said in a husky voice and with a gentle smile, "Go ahead, love." I slowly reached for him and undid his button and zipper. My hands were shaking. I had done this before, just never like this. The others had been anonymous, rough, and hadn't wasted time with blowjobs.

Thibault had total control over me, and he was so gentle about it. Most of the time, I was on the receiving end of things. I had tried to give back because I was all for everyone getting theirs, but a couple of men had gone as far as laughing at me because I wanted to reciprocate or start the loving.

But not him. I took him out of his shorts and jockstrap and looked up again. He rolled a condom on his length, whispering, "I am on PrEP, but better safe than sorry." He rubbed the head of his dick against my mouth. "Open wide, sweetheart." I quickly complied, rewarded with the heavy weight of his cock on my tongue. I licked him from root to tip, tonguing his balls in the process. After a few swipes, I closed my mouth around the head of his cock and sucked gently, eliciting moans from both of us. I slowly went up and down, trying to go as far as I could. It didn't feel like enough.

"Mon Dieu, you are doing great, baby. So good for me." Hearing his praise, I felt bold, and, taking his hands, I pressed them on top of my head. He got the message loud and clear. Holding me in place, still gentle and firm, he moved in and out of my mouth. The noises he made were the hottest things I had ever heard. His moans were deep and getting longer as he went. I used one of my hands to caress his left hip and the other to gently pull and tug at his balls. They were drawing up, so I knew he was close.

He let loose on me, and I gagged, tears streaming to the side of my face. Using my tongue on each upstroke, I pulled back to play with the head of his cock and tongue the slit through the rubber. After a few seconds, I took him as deep as I could. Probably guessing that, though not a novice, I was definitely not skilled enough to deepthroat, he fed me only part of his generous length. But I tried again, gagging more on his dick as I went. He stilled, and his sharp intake of breath and muttered "Merde" told me everything I needed to know. I did it over and over, making more tears fall down my face. As he came, a sweet, drawn-out sigh escaped his lips. I moved back, licking him gently, wishing nothing was between us. Once he was done, he brought me back up and softly, delicately peppered my face, lips, and eyelids with butterfly kisses.

I realized then I was as breathless as he was. I removed the condom and threw it into a wastebasket I could barely see in the corner and put him back inside his shorts while he wiped the tears off my face. That was when I noticed the tears were not only from trying to deepthroat him; they were still flowing. He held me in his arms, rubbing my back in soft circles.

As he was about to speak, we both heard footsteps, giggles, and a whisper-shout of, "Thibault, you there? You rogue."

I took a step back, kissed him gently on the cheek, and left. His whisper of "Wait" and "What's your name?" made me want to stop and go back. But his friends were almost upon us. Blushing, I didn't look at them as I rushed to the bar.

Marcus was sandwiched between a bear and a twink, dancing, and Bobby laughed with a drag queen at the bar. I didn't wait or wave at them and made my way outside. Once at my car, I texted them I was on my way back home so they wouldn't worry.

The one thing running through my mind the whole drive was how getting past this and forgetting it ever happened was going to be the hardest thing in my life.

**2**

———————

THIBAULT

**Thursday, April 11, 2019**

*I* was stacking books at the back of the library, lunchtime almost upon me, when my phone suddenly vibrated in my pocket. I usually wouldn't pick up in the middle of the library but for once decided to go for it. I swiftly moved to the stairs, and up I went into a little alcove. I would have to whisper. I didn't want to disturb anyone who might come in.

"Hey, sister of mine. How are you?"

"Hey, little brother. I am good. You?"

"Things are fine here. What's up?"

"Nothing much. Just wondering how you're doing."

"Did Maman call you and ask you to check on me again?" I asked, slightly exasperated. I knew they meant nothing by it. Even though my mam taught us being single was perfectly fine, she kept asking when I would find someone and settle down. Look up constantly contradicting yourself in the dictionary, and you will find my mother under the definition. Aoibhinn was my sort of sister. She grew up a few streets away from mine and was rejected by her family after coming out. My parents took her in when we were seventeen and we never looked back. I met her when I was five, so my sister of the heart she was. I was used to her and my mam ganging up on me. Especially with us being the same age and her being married.

"Don't be like that, Titi. But come on, you don't go out, and since your 'mystery man'"—I could definitely feel the sarcasm or air quotes here—"last year, you haven't gone to a club or something. Not that it is a relationship. But it's something, at least."

"Oh, vraiment? What do you know about clubs and moving forward? You met your wife in uni in your dorm and knew she was the love of your life. And for your information, I do have a hot date. His name is Aaron. He is thirty, a doctor, and sexy as hell. I am thinking about either blowing him or him blowing me tomorrow night when we go out. There, happy?" There was no hot date, unfortunately. God only knew I wouldn't mind one of those.

"I don't believe you. That sounded a little too easy."

Wait, what? "What do you mean, too easy? Want details? I can tell you about our first date. We dined at the Tavern and had a lovely meal, then walked to my place where we had a drink and gave each other toe-curling orgasms. It was only hand jobs, but the fireworks have me very hopeful for what's next. Definite chemistry."

I heard a loud gasp below me just as my sister laughed and teased me, saying, "You're such a bad liar, little brother. You told me this exact same story six months ago when Mam asked me to give you a pep talk."

While I listened to her laughing at me and telling me to stop being an eejit, I moved toward the banister and saw a quickly retreating figure down the rows of books. The clickety-clack of high heels told me it was a woman, as did the powerful magnolia perfume drifting up toward me.

Ah well, whoever it was, I would either know pretty fast, through gossip or a fight, or I would never know. I hoped for the second option. Nobody needed to know I invented imaginary men to get my mother and sister off my back.

I came back to the conversation because Aoibhinn was chanting my name. "Yes, sorry, I am inside the library and thought I heard someone. Date or no date, Aoibhinn, I need to go. I have my lunch break now, and I can't delay. My colleague won't appreciate it. Enjoy your day. Love you, bye, bye, bye-bye."

"Yeah, okay, bye-bye, bye."

༄

I brought my lunch, except on Thursdays. It became tradition between Sam, George, and me to have lunch together on Thursdays at the Miracle Brew. Our friend Tabitha would sometimes join us. Before I went in, Sam and George were waiting for me outside with a bag of goodies.

"We eating out today?" I asked. Benches were strategically placed along the street under trees in a little park a couple of minutes away from Sam's café.

They both nodded, and we started to leave when a strident voice spoke behind us.

"What about Aaron? Is he not going with you, pervert?" Oh crap. So there had been someone in the library, and it had to have been her. Sally Anne. Between regularly trying to match me up with willing, or more often than not unwilling, women, she was very happy to confront me about my sexuality anywhere, anytime, especially in front of her church cronies.

"I am sorry, Sally Anne, but what are you talking about?" I knew playing innocent wouldn't work, but I had to at least try. It might distract her enough from whatever warpath she was on right now.

"Oh, don't play games with me, Thibault Abrams. You should be ashamed of yourself. Saying such perverted things inside a building where anyone could hear you, especially children. Flaunting your abomination in front of everyone who can see. Dragging others down with you. I will report you to the library and the mayor's office so they can arrest you for such behavior."

"What the hell. I know I shouldn't have talked so crudely inside the library, but it doesn't give you the right to judge me for it. Had I been talking about a woman, you wouldn't have said anything. Just spread the rumor to all who would listen. I was whispering and got carried away. I apologize, especially as none of what I said was true, and there is no Aaron."

She interrupted me, screeching, "Liar. I heard every word you said. What if there were children present? Are you trying to convert everyone around you? Is that how you seduce them?"

I was too shocked to answer. I felt disgusted thinking about it. I always stayed far away from straight men who wanted to experiment. I had seen enough friends getting their hearts, and sometimes other body parts, crushed to know nothing good would come of it.

I took a deep breath, bracing myself. Sam and George were both ready to jump in, but it wouldn't help. It would just be another part of my "gay agenda" to convert the entire population.

"With all due respect, Sally Anne, you went too far with this one. I do not 'convert' people, and I would never go after children. If any child had heard me, I would have apologized to them and their parents. And in fairness, it's not like I went into a very detailed explanation of anything or used particularly dirty words. The fact that you stayed and eavesdropped on the whole conversation is more the problem here than me talking about an imaginary date."

She spluttered and shouted, "You will burn in hell. Our maker will come for you when you least expect it and smite you like he did the people of Sodom and Gomorrah. You will pay for your sins."

On that, she turned around and left us.

Afterward, our lunch was subdued at first until one of us made a joke of the whole encounter, and we relaxed.

## Jack

I tried to stifle a yawn. I wasn't bored much; it had just been one of those long days that felt like they would never end.

I was working with Marcus on one of our cold cases when the chief called me to his office. Where I would have been concerned with my previous boss, with my new one, Chief Christopher Morgan, there was no point speculating. In the past year, he'd called us in to give us good news, shout at us, ask some information on this or that procedure, or simply to chat.

I really enjoyed having him here. Though I was close to the previous chief, I was impressed and happy with his replacement. He fit nicely with us. He didn't try to muscle his way in or treat us like his lackeys and never seemed to have a problem with sexual identity or gender, treating us all as equals, which was a nice change from some of the previous people I'd worked under.

After knocking on his door, I stepped in and waited. He waved me in, gesturing for me to get seated, so I did, fast.

"Tomlins. Let me skip the pleasantries and get to the point. I need you to go assist the police officers in Cottageville. Someone robbed their bank this morning, and they need assistance in retrieving evidence and interviewing witnesses. You know the drill. It shouldn't take you all day, and you can get back to your cold cases with Elmer afterward."

"Of course, sir. Thank you."

I left. There was no point in trying to wiggle out of it. Someone needed to do it, and to be fair to the chief, he tended to rotate us for this kind of help. Though our town was not a city yet, it had grown larger in the past few years, and our precinct had grown too, since crime rose as the town grew. Like this, we had the possibility to help smaller towns around us when needed if no one from the sheriff's office or state departments could assist.

I grabbed my things and stopped by the room where Marcus was still poring over the older case. We both had desks in the bullpen but often used a small out-of-the-way conference room, especially when we needed space to spread out reports and photographs.

"I was voluntold to go assist Cottageville for a bank robbery. I'll catch you later. Worst case, see you tomorrow."

He waved me off, barely looking up. Grabbing my truck, I left for Cottageville. Once there, the officers and I retrieved statements. It was always difficult for the victims and the detective. I understood how horrible, unsettling, and traumatizing this kind of thing could be and tried to be gentle and thoughtful in the way I asked my questions, letting people take their time recounting. But it could quickly turn frustrating as people didn't see or focus on possibly useful details, and by the time I got to my fifth witness, my natural lack of patience showed. I tried to rein it in, but it was always difficult for me. I usually left those types of interviews to Marcus.

By the time we were able to leave the scene and go to the small offices the officer and his chief used, it was late afternoon. We logged the evidence in and I was about to leave when a call came through on their radio. A robbery was taking place at a gas station not ten miles from the city. The description fit the suspects from the bank robbery.

We jumped into our respective cars and arrived as they were walking out of the gas station. The perps tried to run back in, but the door was locked. Afterward, we learned the clerk pressed a button as soon as the robbers left, stranding them outside. Good, we wouldn't face a hostage situation. Only one car was parked off to the side. In a moment of genius, the officer shot two of the tires, making this escape route impossible.

With no car and no way back inside, they went the opposite way, but a couple of warning shots at their feet told them the game was over.

After finishing our arrest, we had to drive back to Weatherboro as we had an interrogation room and the prison. By the time we wrapped up the interrogation, it was late but I was happy this particular crime had solved itself. It wasn't always the case.

By the time I left, most of my colleagues were gone except for two night-shift patrolmen and our night dispatcher.

I made my way home, happy when I remembered I had leftovers from the day before and I didn't need to shop for the next few days. I didn't live far from the precinct and didn't always take my truck. My house was well situated, fifteen minutes on foot from our city center and the police station. The only thing out of the way was my favorite grocery store.

Once home, I set to reheat my food: turkey meatballs,

quinoa, and vegetable stir-fry. I enjoyed the cooking, but on days like today, I was happy to throw everything in the pan to reheat. After securing my gun in the safe and putting my things away, I vegged out on the couch.

My stomach growled at the delicious smells coming from the kitchen. I hurried toward it, and finding the food ready, I plated everything, grabbed cutlery, and made my way back to the sitting room.

After finishing my dinner, I switched off the TV and went upstairs, ready to settle down with a good book. I cleaned myself up, brushed my teeth, settled in bed, and took my e-reader out.

**Friday, April 12, 2019**

I must have fallen asleep without realizing it as I awoke with a start, light still on, e-reader lost somewhere in the tangle of sheet and duvet. Picking up my still-ringing phone, I noticed the time. Barely five thirty in the morning. Whoever was calling at this ungodly hour better have an excellent reason. I picked up the phone and tried my best not to growl. "Detective Tomlins."

"Hi, Detective. This is Dispatch. We have an incident by the duck pond requiring your assistance. Joss was jogging by the reserve and slipped in what looks like blood."

"Gators?"

"We ain't too sure, sir. John is on the scene and requested we call one of the detectives. As you're the one on call for nights this week, it's your turn. John started processing, but we need someone else there."

"Thanks. Please call John and tell him I am on my way. I'll contact him once I arrive, and we will go from there."

"All right, Detective. I'll let him know. Good luck. Holler if I need to dispatch the coroner."

Poppy seeds! This was one way to wake up. Rolling out of bed, I debated taking a shower or going directly. I felt gross, and a shower might help kickstart my body into full awareness. I didn't want to leave John there for too long, but I needed to wake up somehow. I went to the bathroom, stepped in, and put the dial on cooler than usual. I washed, brushed my teeth, slapped on a green shirt and black jeans, grabbed my things, and left.

As this was too early for me to go there on foot, I decided to take the truck. I lived near the back end of the sanctuary, which was more wooded and had only one loop trail. In the opposite direction was the swampy side. The duck pond sat in between. Hoping noise would help wake me up further, I turned on the radio. "Lady Marmalade" came on, and I belted it out in my best voice. Well, off-key and off tempo would be way more accurate, but apart from the birds, there were no witnesses, so at the top of my lungs, I happily sang along. A shimmy here and there completed my performance.

Getting there took me less than five minutes. I arrived at the reserve around 5:45 a.m. and radioed John.

"Hey, man. I am here."

"Sorry, who is it?"

"Detective Tomlins, Officer Woodrow. Six in the duckling morning is not the time to joke, doofus. Is it at the duck pond? Or on a trail?"

"Well, Detective, why don't you get out of the truck?" The knock on my window I definitely should have seen coming startled me. I knew better than to think he wouldn't come round and wait for me. I stepped out of the truck.

"Hey, Johnny. What have you got for me?"

"Follow me. It's right by the duck pond when the trails split."

"All right. Let's go." We started on the trail. The pathway was concrete and lit, but darkness still surrounded us, thanks to the dense tree and bush population.

"It's so weird, Jack. I can't figure out what happened there. The blood could be animal or human, and there is lots of it. If it's animal, then it's a big one. I thought a gator might have snatched whatever it was, but they don't come in far enough. And I didn't see the usual drag marks."

"What did you do with Joss?"

"I took his statement, then walked him back to my car. He was covered in blood, so I handed him my spare clothes and bagged his. I took pictures both at the site and in the parking lot—better lighting. As far as I can tell, he slipped in the blood, as it was on his back and nowhere else. I sent him home. He should be by the station today on his lunch break to check his statement and complete it, if he remembers anything else."

We arrived at the scene, marked with yellow tape and evidence flags. Before we moved farther, I stopped John. Lowering myself, I pulled on a pair of gloves. "Evidence bag?" He handed me one quickly. I grabbed a small box of matches. Few people used them nowadays, and it might be irrelevant. As I crouched there, I saw something small near the matches. It was white and brown, rough to the touch. I asked for a second bag, then dropped whatever it was inside. "Can you place an evidence flag here? And take pictures?" I placed the bags on the ground where I had taken the evidence.

I strode back to the blood. It had dried except in the center where it pooled.

"Did you get samples?" I inquired.

"Not yet. I secured the scene and then walked back to the parking lot to wait for you and grab flashlights." Dawn was breaking, and the streetlamps along the path illuminated the scene but not enough. He handed me one light, and we both looked closer.

"Apart from Joss, did you step in it or notice anyone else?"

"No, why? What do you see?"

I pointed with my flashlight to a streak of blood and two handprints and footprints. Moving around the puddle to the right, I shifted my light to the other side, revealing a different set of marks, this time only the front of a shoe. I brought the beam of light toward us, and there, very faint, were more steps, fading right behind us.

Giving the light to John and using flags and markers from the kit he had left a little way off the direct path, I marked the steps from right behind where we stood to the puddle, where they were more visible. Standing next to John again, two distinct sets were now visible. Only Joss's footsteps were visible on the right side, removing all trace of anyone else. If there was someone else.

I grabbed the light and placed myself at the start of the footsteps, moving next to them. Walking bent forward wasn't the easiest for a man my size, but I hit the jackpot, spotting blood drops about two to three feet away from them. The bushes and grass across from me appeared bent. It looked the same to my right. So, most likely two people holding someone or something that was dripping blood between them. The path was about four feet wide, with grass and bushes on both sides, for a total of six feet. Some bushes were thorny, so people generally kept to the path and barely anyone strayed to the grass.

"Start photographing what we have. I am going to follow that blood trail." I walked beside the trail and placed my markers as I went. Noticing after a few minutes I would soon run out, I grabbed sticks from the bushes. I placed them near the blood drops to save a few flags in case we needed to highlight anything else. At the parking lot, the trail led to a parking spot. The ground was sandy and earth was displaced but nothing we would be able to use to check tire tracks. Not that tracks would tell us much, unless the car had special tires with the name of the owner on them... One could dream.

Making sure I didn't step on anything, I traced my steps back to John. I let him finish taking pictures and started bagging samples of blood, earth, grass, and the shoe imprints. Between the two of us, the evidence was in John's car before seven thirty. We did a wider search but saw nothing else. If it wasn't for the blood drops, I would have searched the whole sanctuary, calling in reinforcements to cover more ground, but decided against it. I would see if anything turned up this morning. If no calls came through, I would take Marcus with me and search the area.

Either way, the day promised to be long.

**3**

---

THIBAULT

**Still Friday**

*I* couldn't breathe. "Born This Way" rustled through the surrounding leaves. I couldn't move. I needed to move.

I sat bolt upright in my bed.

Lady Gaga kept singing in my ear while I struggled to slow down my breathing and soothe my racing heart. I dreamed about bleeding on the forest floor, nothing else but trees and a retreating figure.

What a splendid start to my day. It wasn't the first time I'd had this dream, and I dreaded it. It normally had more details, but my alarm had woken me up before it had gotten that far. I didn't believe in dreams particularly, but this one always rattled me. I was thankful it didn't happen often.

I switched off my alarm and started the radio on my phone while shuffling toward the bathroom. The riff of an eighties rock song filled the air, making my heart thump and adrenaline flow through me for an excellent reason this time. After a brisk shower and express grooming, I put on dark slacks, my light purple shirt, and fun socks (today's choice: pink ducks on black).

Needing a boost for the day, I put on eyeliner. I used navy blue, which didn't complement my hazel eyes like my gold one but fit well with the purple. And it didn't clash with my dark brown hair or pale skin. Working as a librarian had its perks. I needed to be presentable, but I still could be myself. Most people seemed fine with my being gay. There was the occasional frown, especially on days I wore eyeliner at work, but most were getting used to it or pretended to in front of me. A very select few still sneered at it or commented, but I let that go.

I had tried dates with the few eligible men available around here, but nothing came of it. Where I didn't find a lover or a boyfriend, though, at least I gained friends. Only one man had stood me up. We met through an app, and I'd had the impression he might be in the closet. When I tried to reach out to him after our missed date, he made excuses but soon after ghosted me. I deleted the app, not having found what I was looking for.

I made my way downstairs, wondering how the day would play out. I hated waking up from a nightmare; I always felt unsettled afterward. Once in the kitchen, I realized I didn't have coffee or anything qualifying as breakfast food. I took a pen and paper and wrote my grocery list, adding a reminder on my phone. I always kept making lists, just to forget all about them later.

As I turned around, a loud meow followed by swats to my arm and leg made me jump. The cats were inside. Thank god the one thing I always made sure I bought was cat food. And dog food. And feed or grain for the rest of the animals.

I inherited the zoo, as I liked to call it, at the same time I inherited the house. It was a big part of my decision to stay, stealing my heart right from the beginning. So was my first impression of this wonderful old house. When I walked into its giant kitchen, I fell in love with it. It also had a sitting room and living room, laundry room, and a small bath downstairs. Upstairs were four bedrooms, one en suite bathroom in what had been the master bedroom when Ruth lived here but was now a guest room, and one main bathroom.

The attic was big enough to convert into a bedroom, or like the idea I'd toyed with, a studio for my yoga and meditation. Or a library. I couldn't make up my mind. Last but not least was a large basement with only a heater and empty space. I thought about converting it into a gym, but I would not use it enough. One day, if I had children, it could be a fun room for teenagers.

The house sat on an extensive property with farming lands that had been in Ruth's husband's family for a few generations. Unfortunately, David, Ruth's husband, hadn't had any surviving nephews or nieces, and they'd never had children. Lucky for me.

On the suggestion of Steve, the farmhand who fed the animals and who I met that first day two years ago, I reached out to the surrounding neighbors, and three jumped at the opportunity to cultivate parts of the land again. I struck agreements with them: low rent in exchange for some fodder for the animals.

That worked wonders and helped me, in part, to integrate better in town. My great-aunt Ruth was quite the character and in equal parts loved and feared by the town's people. Trying to fill those shoes was daunting, so I never bothered, instead creating a nice little space for myself in this magical place.

The sharp bite of teeth on my calf and the swat to my

backside brought me back to the present. I fed the wild beasts before I ended up being their breakfast. Leaving the three cats to their food, I exited the house to feed the rest of the zoo. I had two gorgeous dogs, a few chickens with different species mingling together, a donkey, a pig, and two goats.

Taking care of them was more relaxing than I'd thought, and I took pleasure in it on the weekends when the labor of cleaning their pens gave me time to think. I learned fast that having a farm and farm animals was more work than I'd imagined. After I moved in, Steve stayed and tended to the zoo every day except for feedings and the weekends, when I would take care of things myself.

While I fed the animals, I realized I'd never received a letter yesterday. I started receiving letters almost a year and a half ago, at first once a month and more recently every week. Always on Thursdays, with no stamp, return address, or anything else on them. Just my name on the envelope and a few words inside it. I had considered for a hot second if my mystery man and my secret admirer were the same man but quickly dismissed it. I met Mystery Man at Pride in Charleston and that man was sweet—the one from the letters wasn't.

I was so absorbed in my thoughts, I spent longer feeding the animals than usual. The task done, I rushed inside, changed shoes, grabbed the essentials, and hurried to my car. I wasn't late, but if I planned to grab coffee and breakfast on the way, I didn't have much time.

I drove to town, taking the 303, then followed the boulevard to Hampton Street and parked at the library. It was a tiny town with a couple main intersections and a cute center. I was accustomed to one main street in most towns this size in Ireland. Getting used to not saying main street when I meant the one the library was on was a bit of a change.

From there, I made my way to the Miracle Brew. As I

opened the door, it moved away from me, and I stumbled into the broad chest of the man holding it wide open. I froze, inhaling lemon, mandarin orange, and sandalwood. That scent meant only one thing: Detective Joyful. When I'd arrived in town, I discovered two things fast. First, the detectives were hot as hell, and second, this particular one had taken an instant dislike to me. I tried to ask why, but he shut me down. In fairness, the way I'd talked the first time we met had been a disaster. I wouldn't have let myself speak any further the second time either.

Jack Tomlins was six feet four inches of muscled goodness. He had dark green eyes, dirty blond hair, and a short, well-trimmed beard shot through with a little silver. His tanned skin made his green eyes look at once deeper and brighter. He was always impeccable, whether in his civilian clothes or what I liked to think of as his detective's uniform, which consisted today of a dark green shirt and black pants. That never distracted me from how handsome he was or his delightful body. He brought out my evil side, and I would love nothing more than mussing his neat look.

He always smelled heavenly, at least to me, his aftershave mixing up with warm sunshine and all male. Not that I made a habit of sniffing him. I had an inkling he would take offense. I was always gravitationally challenged, and the most spectacular occurrences had the tendency to happen around him. In the past two years, I had bumped into him more times than I could count.

"Oopsy daisy. Detective, if all you wanted was a hug, you could ask. Trust me, I am all for it. Anytime, all the time," I said with a cheeky smile.

I looked up as he took a step back. He towered over me, as I was only five feet seven to his six-feet-four-inch frame. And here was the almighty scowl. I still hadn't figured out if it was a default setting or if I was the special person bringing it out.

"Mr. Abrams. I would say it's a pleasure, but then again, lying is not my thing."

Another impressive start.

"Thibault, Detective. Mr. Abrams is my dad. I think after two years, you are allowed to use my first name. What more needs to happen between us before you do?"

"You moving out of my way would be a brilliant start. My morning has been bad enough without you making it any worse than it needs to be."

*Hell, Detective, who pissed in your cornflakes this morning* was on the tip of my tongue. I bit it back. It wouldn't help, not that being nice ever did either. But there was no point fueling the fire.

I stepped around him, and looking over my shoulder on my way to the counter, I quipped, "Well, if that was all it took, you should have said so a long time ago. I started wondering if you needed an engraved invitation. So from now on, Jack and Thibault it is." I took a breath and couldn't help myself. In a voice that was coming from god only knew where, I intoned, "Ta-dam. Congratulations, you have now reached level two in the relationship. You can achieve the next level through getting coffee together, having an actual conversation, or even a handshake. Good luck."

The eye roll was new. The growled "God give me patience" wasn't.

As he stepped out, I said, "And a delightful day to you too, Detective."

I turned toward the counter and noticed all eyes on me. As it was before eight o'clock, that meant not too many eyes but enough to make me blush. I hoofed it to the counter, trying to ignore everyone else to reach my friend, who was standing near the coffee machine.

"Heya, Sam, looking good this morning."

Samuel Jasper Clarington, as I discovered on one drunken night, was one of my closest friends. He was tall, at least six feet two, and very fit. His features were striking. His mother was from Argentina, and his dad had roots in the Nordic countries. He got her dark honey coloring and his father's light brown eyes and honey blond hair. Right now, he looked at me like I had grown a second head.

"Good morning to you too, sunshine. What in the high heavens was that?"

"What do you mean?"

"What do you mean, what do I mean? Are you joking? You are always so nice and sweet to everyone you meet. Even the people that try to get a rise out of you, like the ladies from church, do not fire you up that much. What is it with you and Jack? He is not always the smiliest guy out there, but this is next level with you."

"Yeah, I noticed." I sighed. "I have no clue what it is. He brings something snarky and sassy out in me. After that first horrendous encounter with him here, we kept pushing each other's buttons to the max. When I see him, it's like this devil side of me comes out to play. I can't help it. You know how it goes."

"No, I wouldn't know." He seemed to study me for a second, then added, "But it's fun to see this side of you. Now, apart from your café au lait, what would you like, sweet cheeks?"

"I would kill for a chocolate chip and cherry scone, if you have any today."

"Sure, no problem. Coming right up." He turned around, writing my name and order on a little paper and sticking it on my favorite to-go cup, which I happily surrendered to him. He cashed me out before handing me one of the best treats out there. I loved their chocolate and orange peel ones, but the cherry scones hit me just right on a morning like this.

"By the way," Sam continued, "did you hear the latest? Jack was here after quite the night, a little bird told me."

"Ooooh, do tell. If he is getting some, it might make him a little more palatable. Please, pretty, pretty please, say you got raunchy details?" Then again, seeing his reaction this morning, probably not.

A throat cleared right behind me, and I blushed. In times like these, I cursed my mam's ancestors; I loved my pale skin and wasn't too unhappy with my freckles, but boy, did I hate the way I turned red.

"Jack, what can I get you?" Sam inquired, trying so hard not to laugh.

"Sorry, needed to grab the list. I would like two black coffees, two cappuccinos, one latte, and one caramel macchiato to go. And if you have some blueberry or chocolate muffins, about six of them would be perfect, thank you."

"Well, it must have been quite the fun night you had, Detective, if you need that much coffee and carbs to recover," I joked. By the looks of his order, he was feeding half the police station.

He looked at me as if I was day-old gum melted on the sidewalk on a scorching day that he had stepped on, and he'd had just about enough of it all.

"What are you going on about now?" he asked, exasperated. Had I misunderstood what Sam told me? My mind had a tendency to picture Jack in the sexiest ways, and the thought of him and anything happening at night sent my brain down a naughty path. Simply imagining the things he could have gotten up to last night to be so cranky this morning had me growing hot.

"Well, Sammy here was telling me all about your sinful evening."

Sam blushed and jumped in. "All I said was, 'He had quite the night.' It is not my fault your dirty brain jumped to such conclusions." Oops. Confirmed. I definitely misunderstood. Me and my dirty mind.

"Here is your order, Thibault. Detective, it will be another minute," one of Sam's employees called out.

I looked at my watch. Still ten minutes before I would be anywhere near being late. Well, late for me. I had until eight thirty to open the library. I preferred being there before or around eight. It gave me the opportunity to check everything was in order and a little quiet time to get in the right frame of mind for the day. My job was fantastic, but it could be taxing. Not as hard as working full time in the coffee shop, but dealing with any kind of customers could be difficult.

I grabbed my coffee and looked back at Jack and Sam. Both glowered at me. Sam I could understand, since we got caught gossiping, but the detective I didn't. What was he upset about now?

We all stared at each other for a couple of awkward minutes. The barista called out to Jack, who grabbed his gigantic order of coffee and sweet treats, then left without a backward glance.

I turned to Sam. "Was it something I said?" When all else failed, go for the innocent look.

"From what I know, it could be a bit of you and a lot of last night's events. There was an incident early this morning. A jogger—I think Joss, you know, the guy from the bank, but I am not sure—was running on a trail near the wildlife sanctuary when he slipped in what seems to be blood, and quite a bit of it. Not sure what happened last night. I just heard they finished late."

"Ah, so that's the kind of night you were talking about. Well, explains why he was in such a great mood and happy to run into me this morning. I am guessing you didn't learn the details from the man himself?"

"Nope, from George. Tabitha got the info this morning when she went to drop him his coffee."

The source was reliable. He was tight-lipped in most cases, but the ladies knew how to get a little something out of him. Get him properly fed or flustered, and you would learn the best information. He didn't overshare, just enough for the tongues to wag. We sometimes got some more details during our Thursday lunches, but rarely.

"Well, if it comes from George, we can trust it. He might dish more out to us later." I smiled.

"Most likely," answered Sam. "But wanna know the most intriguing and scary part of all this?"

"Sure, shoot." I shrugged. In for a penny, in for a pound.

"There was no body." He started whispering, and I found myself half leaning over the counter.

"Really. Was it gators?"

"It might well be. George didn't give up anything else. I'll ask Joss if I see him later on his lunch break. I am guessing there is something more to it. Tabitha said he looked like he expected things to get bad. We will see what they can find."

Tabitha and George were quite close, and I enjoyed getting to know her. She was sweet and worked in a boutique that sold antiques and high-end clothing. She and Sam were my go-to sources for gossip.

"Well, I've got to go, but if you catch anything else interesting, I can pop back around for a chat at lunchtime." I turned toward the door. "Have a brilliant day, guys," I called out over my shoulder.

"You too, Thibault," came the chorused reply.

I made my way outside and toward the library. Only a five-minute walk, and the sun felt warm on this beautiful spring day. The smell of coffee and sugar wafted through the air, mixing with warm earth and car smells. The breeze, cooling me down a little, made the leaves rustle.

I said hello to a couple friendly faces. After a while here, people warmed up to you. It had taken a little over six months for people to see me as part of the town. By now most people in Weatherboro knew my face, thanks to working in such a central place as the library and going to the market twice a month. It had helped me carve out a place here, and it felt like home.

I enjoyed going to work every day. Well, I had my down days like everybody else, but it never was about work. Seeing people there, old and young, getting lost in the stories we helped them find within our walls was a pleasure I reveled in.

Looking at the time, I realized that strolling was not the best plan and sped up. I rushed up the stairs on the left side of the library where the workers' entrance and break room were situated. It was an imposing old brick building, all one floor with a huge basement underneath, large windows, and ornate glass doors we secured with wood shutters every evening. The back entrance was less intricate, just a simple red wood door. I put the key in and turned it. Unlocked. Weird. Gwendolyn had closed yesterday, and I knew for a fact she would never leave it open. We all had become very careful following the break-in. Gwen was not the kind to forget; she was too anxious.

I opened the door anyway, which, as usual, stuck after a few inches. I pulled until it opened fully. Taking my phone out and entering 911 just in case, I crept inside.

I switched on the lights and placed my coffee and treats on the table closest to me. The break room was not very large but spacious enough for a long counter with a small fridge, microwave, sink, and cupboards holding everything we might need. There were four round tables with comfortable chairs, all done in tones of gray and lilac, very relaxing. I made my way to the corridor and turned right toward the primary room of the library and the front desk. In the opposite direction sat two offices, one small one with a couch and a recording desk for the camera we installed outside, and the office of Charlene, our director.

The weirdest smell hit my nose, sickly sweet mixed with something metallic.

Pressing the green button on my phone, I turned the corner and got a full view of the front door and desk. She was sitting on the counter, reclining. I made my way toward her, bile hitting the back of my throat. Once I was eight feet away, I stopped. I had seen enough.

My call connected. "Nine-one-one, what is your emergency?"

"Hi. My name is Thibault Abrams. I am at the library in Weatherboro, and I am pretty sure I found a body?"

"Sir, could you please give me the address?"

I provided it to her, sweat trickling down my spine and cold shivers running through me.

"What did you say the emergency was?"

"I just came in to work. There is a woman here, and I am pretty sure she is dead."

"Alright, sir. A team will be with you shortly. Don't go anywhere."

The phone clattered to the floor as I turned around, staggered forward, and vomited in the closest potted plant, barely hearing the dispatcher calling out to me through the phone.

**Jack**

John left for the station, and I offered to do a coffee run, singing along to "Party in the U.S.A." on my way to the Miracle Brew. It wasn't our only coffee shop in town but definitely was the best. One of my old schoolmates Sam bought and renamed it about five years ago when the owner retired. Sam made the best scones and muffins in the state. Well, at least that was how they tasted to me.

I'd wanted to make this quick, but between forgetting to check with the precinct for their orders and running smack-dab into one of the most infuriating men I knew, it took longer than expected.

On my way to the station, I still felt a mix of exasperation and unexpected mirth, which was usually the case after any encounter I had with Thibault Abrams. He was a weird mix of shy, snarky, and adorable. Well, with me, he was all snark, which would come out full force if he knew I thought of him as *adorable.*

If I was honest, I enjoyed our encounters most times, though I was always very careful not to let him see it. But today I simply couldn't cope. Between the lack of sleep and that puzzling scene, hearing him gossip about me had been the last straw, and it wasn't even eight in the morning. I had been especially rude today, but let's face it, I wasn't ever nice to him. I didn't think he would notice the difference.

I wish he'd been right, that I was coming back from one hell of a fun night. I was not sure I'd ever had a night that would qualify as his idea of fun. The glimpse I'd had of a good time last year had left me wanting more. I'd never gone for it, though. Seeing how he acted around me, I wasn't sure he would be open to the idea. And I wasn't prepared for the consequences. I was out, but saying it was a whole other ball game to being in a relationship everyone could see.

Leaving my treasures at the front desk, I went into the station. George, our receptionist, hollered for the team to come and get their coffees and treats. I took my black coffee and nabbed a chocolate chip and orange muffin as I went to my desk. Bless those men for putting one of my favorite muffins in the order. I didn't indulge often, so it was nice to see they'd noticed.

I recounted to Marcus the events of yesterday and this morning, and we talked about what his day had entailed before deciding which cold case to work on next. Barely fifteen minutes had passed when George came barreling through.

Breathless, he told us, "Dispatch just received a call from Thibault."

"What's wrong, George?" I asked, unsettled.

"He found a body at the library. There was a clatter on the phone, and the line was still open, but the dispatcher can't hear anyone or anything on the other side."

My heart dropped to my stomach.

I stood up, starting for the entrance, Marcus hot on my heels and hollering, "John, we need to go to the library now. Thibault Abrams found the body. George, call the coroner and tell him to meet us there, please."

As one, we rushed out of the door.

**Friday April 12th 2019 - Still**

After my stomach stopped revolting, I made my way back outside, trying not to touch anything. I shouldn't have gone inside, but for some reason, I went against my gut instinct. I should have known, shouldn't I?

I rushed down the stairs and slid down the wall next to them, sitting on the warm ground. To keep from hyperventilating, I put my head between my legs. I was so absorbed in my breathing that a hand brushing my hair away from my face made me scream.

I looked up, trying to scramble away. When I realized who it was, I stopped. "Jack," I said, breathing hard.

"Hey," he whispered, crouching to my level. "Sorry for scaring you. I called your name three times, but you didn't move or seem to notice, and I was afraid..." He stopped midsentence, swallowed, then continued. "You all right, Thibault? What happened? Son of a firestarter, you scared the blazes out of me when I was told you called but the dispatcher couldn't get you back on the phone."

I noticed my empty hands. "I am sorry. I must have dropped it before I..."

"Before you what?" he prompted.

"Um, puked. God, I feel so gross right now, and I can still smell that awful perfume and see her. Why is this happening? Why is she here? Who is it? Is she dead? What's going on, Jack?"

"You puked?" he repeated, somewhat puzzled. What he found weird about the idea was anyone's guess.

"Not on your crime scene, Detective, in one of our potted plants. That's all you heard in my word vomit?" *Vomit* and *puke* were the winning words of the day.

He looked at me with a soft smile on his lips. "There you are," was all he said.

We stared at each other until someone said, "Um, Jack, we will check out what's going on, all right?" Two people in uniform and someone who I was pretty sure was the coroner stood behind him, but I couldn't quite make out their faces. Things were blurry.

"The... um,"—I swallowed—"the body is inside, front desk." When I saw them go to the front entrance, I called out to them. "It's still closed. You can use the side entrance, which is right here." I pointed to the door to my right. They all turned as one, went up the stairs, and disappeared inside.

I made to move, but Jack stopped me, placing his hand on my shoulder.

"Yes, Detective? I just want to show them where to go and retrieve my phone."

"That's all right, Thibault," he replied gently. "They know where they are going. If they can't find the front desk, then we have a serious problem. Let's get you up and seated in my car."

I followed him, not too sure what to do with myself anyway. I noticed then that, despite being close by, they had come in their trucks, which were now blocking the front of the library. I debated telling him about parking at the back, but it wouldn't matter. On TV shows, investigations always took a while, and I had the feeling the library would not open today —or tomorrow, for that matter.

"I need to call Charlene. She and Nathaniel come in later on Fridays, as I am the one opening up. Do you know when we can reopen?"

"A couple days at best. A little longer, depending on how much we find straightaway. Cleanup will add another day, depending on when someone can come here." Well, wasn't that just great?

"Tell you what, let me see where the guys are at. It will give you a few minutes to call Charlene and get yourself sorted. Here is my phone. Her number should be under Char." He gazed at me with kind eyes. What I wouldn't give for him to look at me the same way under different circumstances.

"Thanks, Detective." Seated inside his car, I dialed Charlene while watching him walk away and disappear around the corner of the library as the call connected.

"Charlene? This is Thibault."

"Thibault, sweetie, what can I do for you? Everything fine at the library? Why does this say Jack's phone if you're the one calling me?"

I swallowed hard.

"Well, I arrived a couple minutes before eight and stumbled on a dead body. Not literally, but yeah, dead body. Um, the police are here. Jack said it would take two days or more before we reopen."

"Oh my god, sweetie. Are you okay?" she exclaimed.

"I am fine, I think. I am not sure. Physically, I am grand.

The rest, I don't know. Jack went to check what is going on, and I will then have to give my statement, I guess. He didn't say. Could you please ring Nathaniel to let him know? My phone is inside, and I am not sure when I'll get it back."

"Do you want me to come now, Thibault?" she questioned, always so sweet.

"Nah, that's fine, Ms. C. No point for both of us to be in the police's way. They might need you later, though. I'll ask the detectives to call you if that's the case. Or call you back when I know more."

"Ok, Thibault, keep me posted, dear. I'll come around at my normal time if I don't hear from you before then."

"Sounds good, Ms. C. Talk to you later." Feeling a little better, I hung up. Charlene's voice always soothed me.

I then settled down in the car and waited.

❧

## Jack

I trudged away from the car. Seeing him on the floor had done something to me. The panic and dread coursing through me weren't like anything I'd ever felt before. When the phone dropped, a million scenarios had run through my head, and seeing him there, folded in on himself, my heart stopped. I just wanted to draw him into me and never let go.

I went inside where Thibault suggested and found myself in the staff room. It looked the same as before. Voices echoed from further inside, so I followed the sound. The closer I got, the more I could smell it: blood, a cloying perfume, and sick.

Fudge berries. Exactly what we needed. This was shaping up to be one hell of a day. I arrived in the main room and found the guys working on the scene. The phone on the floor had to be Thibault's. I told the dispatcher we were there and hung up. Four feet from it to its right was a potted plant covered in vomit.

I put on a pair of gloves from my kit, grabbed markers, and placed one next to the phone and one in front of the potted plant. Someone would spot the phone, but the puke was unlikely unless they knew to look for it.

I moved toward the front desk where our coroner had started his exam. The front room was spacious, with shelves to my right and tables spread around with comfortable chairs. On the left, the room opened, filled with shelves and more tables. The front desk was almost in front of me. On opposite sides of the room were two sets of stairs leading to a long balcony. Surrounding the room were more books and reading nooks. The furniture, stairs, and floor were all in rich mahogany tones, and the walls were a fresh cream color on which hung some brilliant paintings and watercolors from artists in town.

The woman was propped on the desk; her pale limbs were stiff, but she looked as if she was reclining with her left elbow propped on the side of the desk and her right hand placed next to her hip. Her head was forward, and her long dark hair covered her face. She had on a pretty dress of soft pink and dark blue, the skirt stopping under the knee in her reclining position. Black stains marked her chest and the skirt. The rest of her seemed untouched. Whoever had put her there did so with some care.

"Hope you took pictures of that first, Doc?" I knew he probably had. Reginald was a portly gentleman with neatly coiffed salt-and-pepper hair, in his early fifties, and our coroner. He shared his time between his office at the station and the funeral parlor, where he was a qualified mortician. Sometimes, in his need to make sure we treated the victims right, he rushed to them before doing the basic steps like taking pictures and placing markers on anything around the body. Eyebrows raised, he looked toward me. I lifted my hands and shrugged. I had to ask, though I knew Marcus kept a close eye on him when I couldn't.

He smiled and answered. "Hey, Detective. Nice of you to join this little party. You and I both know I can be forgetful, but this differs somewhat from your usual accidental or medical deaths. I took the pictures. There is nothing around the body I could disturb, so I started on our victim here."

Standing right next to him, I couldn't see the face of the woman, but my gut told me it would be someone I knew. I wasn't looking forward to it. It was never easy, but knowing the person, especially with a violent death, made it that much harder and somehow personal whether or not you were close to them. Though murder wasn't common, we saw death around these parts every now and again. It always felt like a punch to the gut. The smells and sights I could wrap my head around but not how someone's life had ended, especially when that end came abruptly for someone young. Talking with our previous chief before he'd retired, I'd learned it didn't get any easier as you grew older.

I called out to Marcus so he could join us for what Reginald had to say.

"Do you have anything for us, Reginald, or is it too soon to tell?" I quizzed.

"Well, I can give you the bare facts. My actual findings I'll provide later," he replied, shrugging. Yes, we all knew the drill here, no matter how hard it could get sometimes.

"Sounds fair to me." He turned back toward the body, and so did I.

"Female, mid-forties to mid-fifties. She has a nasty wound to the neck. It will need a proper examination, of course, but I would say the artery was torn, maybe during a struggle. She lost the blood wherever she was. I am not sure if they killed her here or somewhere else, but seeing the wound and how spotless this place is even though I don't smell bleach, I would bet on it not happening here.

"I see defensive wounds to her arms. Rigor mortis has set in, and body temperature is seventy-five, so I would say estimated time of death between eight and twelve hours ago. If one of you can confirm with the library people what temperature they keep it here during the night, that would help me narrow it down. I am going to pack and bring her back to the station with me."

"One more thing, Doc—did you find anything to identify her?"

Reginald looked at me, then back at the body. He shook his head and replied, "No, there is no handbag or wallet around or on her person. But..."

Trailing off, he simply lifted the hairs away from her face, and Marcus and I both gasped. "Sally Anne!"

"It looks like it, yes. I grew up with her. As horrible as she could get, she didn't deserve this."

"Agreed, Doc. Thanks for that."

I looked at Marcus, "You okay continuing here while I take Thibault's statement or you want to do it?" I would much prefer handling him, but we split duties as much as we could. As senior detective, I was usually in charge, but I considered us partners and equals, especially at crime scenes.

"I am fine, man. I'll keep processing things with John. You talk to Thibault. Just be gentle for once, please. I know you two get on each other's nerves, but I have the feeling you will get more out of him than I would if you tread carefully."

I made my way toward the back stairs. I might need to ask Thibault to unlock the front door so moving the body would be easier. I stopped as it dawned on me that, though easier, it would attract more attention we didn't need. As it was, this would be all over town before sunset.

I went back inside and asked Reginald, "I know it's steeper, but do you think you could manage the back stairs? It would attract a lot less notice, and we might contain things better, at least until we can contact next of kin."

John and Marcus stepped forward. "Don't worry, Jack. We will bring her down."

I made my way back outside. Inside my truck, Thibault hunched in on himself, trying to make himself invisible. This was highly unusual for him. Though not necessarily the life of the party at all times, he was nice and polite with everyone, outgoing even. Not the hiding or defeated type. But where he was sweet if somewhat distant with most people, he was different around me. I hoped his natural sassiness would come out to play and help him through the next few minutes, enough for him to recount what had happened.

I opened the door to the driver's side of the truck and stepped in. Thibault seemed in a daze. His usually beautiful hazel eyes were red and unfocused, panicked, and his breathing was ragged. "Hey, Thibault, it's only me. Jack, remember? You're in my car. I need you to take deep breaths. Breathe with me for a bit. Can you do that for me, sweetheart?" He nodded. I hoped he would not notice the endearment I had just used. I took deep breaths, happy to see he was doing the same. Closing the door softly behind me, I settled in.

I shouldn't have left him alone in the car for so long. Some people were stopping to stare. A few were moving on, but we were attracting a crowd. I called the station. "Hey George, could you please send us someone to do crowd control? Yes, anyone you can find. As long as they help people move along. Great, thank you."

I turned back to Thibault. "I am sorry I left you alone. Do you feel well enough to answer a few questions?"

He blinked at me a few times, looked down at his hands, and then cleared his throat and whispered, "Sure, Detective. Go ahead."

That wouldn't do. If I wanted to get anything coherent, I needed him fully there. "You can call me Jack. We went up one level this morning. You can't go back on that. Especially after all we have been through together. The doorway encounters, the dancing around each other, your incessant need to hug me..." I trailed off and waited for a reaction, rewarded with a snort and a twinkle in his eyes.

"Sure, Jack. I need the hugs. Let's go with that."

I pulled out my notebook. "All joking aside, could you please tell me what happened? Maybe start from after I saw you at the coffee shop. Is it okay if I take notes and record this conversation?"

He handed me my phone back and swallowed. "Right. Sure, go ahead."

I switched on the recording app on my phone and took out my notebook. To show I was ready, I waved at him and nodded.

"Once you left the shop, I chatted with Sam a couple more minutes, then made my way to the library. We open at eight thirty every day except Saturdays, and we are closed on Sundays. I arrived at the side door, as that's the one we always use for opening and closing. It gives us the freedom to take our time prepping and making sure everything is fine before we open the main doors. I put the key in and was about to turn it when I noticed it was unlocked. This was weird, as we always make sure it's locked, especially after the break-in. A few people have the key to the side door, but only Charlene and I have the keys for the front door. It didn't look forced, and nothing was disturbed. I took out my phone and pulled up the number for the police station, just in case. And then I went in.

"I left my coffee and food on the table closest to the door. I had a weird feeling, but I forged on. I slowly made my way towards the front desk. Just before I stepped into the front room, I registered a powerful smell. Like potent flower perfume, cloying, with an underlying smell of rot? Or something metallic? I don't know; it was weird. When I turned the corner, I didn't compute what my eyes were seeing. But it didn't take long. I started getting closer—I am not sure why. To see who it was, I guess, or ask her if she needed help. Then I noticed the blood on her neck and clothes. That's when I called you. The rest is hazy. I think my phone dropped, and I just needed to expel whatever was in my stomach. I made my way outside right after and waited for you to arrive."

While he told his story, he retreated into himself some more, making himself as small a target as possible. A little more and he would disappear into my upholstery. Seeing death, especially one so shocking, was hard on anyone. As seasoned as we were in law enforcement, I had seen how it could affect us, no matter how long we had been in this business. I wouldn't say we got used to it, but over time you learned to shield yourself, and most times when we got on scene, we braced ourselves for what we'd find there.

He'd had no warning and, unless he had been present for the death of one of his grandparents, parents, or a friend, then he had never seen a dead body before. At least not one outside of a coffin. I just hoped the crash would come for him while I was around. I knew we weren't anything to each other because I had never let it happen, but I couldn't walk away today. It would hit him all at once, and he would need someone there. And for some unknown reason, I felt it needed to be me.

"Thanks, Thibault. Do you remember touching anything? The doorknob, the door, shelves, anything else?"

He looked confused, then licked his lips, "The doorknob. I might have grabbed the side of the door, as it sticks a little sometimes."

"Do you know if anyone else does that too?" I queried.

**5**

---

THIBAULT

**Still Friday**

*I* wasn't sure how long I stared at him. I needed to get a grip, but it was so hard. What had he asked again? "Um, I guess everyone who ever used the side door would have had to pull it at least once. Everyone at the library leaves it closed once we are in. And we all use it instead of the front, even when it's open. We open the door and leave it propped up for the deliverymen. That's the only time we would use the doorstopper, as the wind closes it when it's blowing the right way, unlike today."

"Anyone else?" he pushed, taking notes.

"Anyone with a key. Charlene can give you more details, but I would say anyone from the HPS, the Historical Preservation Society. We are here for anyone else who wants to hold a forum, course, et cetera. They are the only ones allowed to use the library outside of hours. The previous lady who was chair of the committee was working part-time at the library, and that's how it started, from what I understand."

His kind eyes were starting to undo me, so I faced the front. Merde, I shouldn't have. People were looking in our direction, wondering what had happened. I was not looking forward to the scrutiny, the questions, the gossip. I mean, for all my blustering around the man sitting next to me, I wasn't much of a people person. Oh, I was sociable to a certain extent, but it worked better when I hid in the crowd. I loved dance classes with my mam, but I hated being the center of attention, so I did my best to stay out of the way. Same with my yoga classes. One-on-one interactions were fine. The library was the only place I relished being center stage. It might have been because books made me confident, or I got so lost in my love for them and trying to get people to fall in love with them too, I didn't notice I was talking to actual people.

This was so much worse than dance classes or talking about books, wasn't it? Fuck, thinking about it made me sweat bullets. I wouldn't have Maman to run interference. Before I rolled further down my spiral of oh-so-joyful thoughts, Jack put his hand on my arm.

"Sorry, Detective, you were saying?" I said, still avoiding his eyes.

"Don't worry. I have a couple more preliminary questions. Once we are done, we can schedule a proper interview at the station for tomorrow. How does that sound?"

I shuddered, shook my head, and tried to concentrate. "Sure thing, Detective. What do you need?"

I hoped he would get on with it so I might go home. On second thought, maybe not. I definitely didn't want to be alone. Maybe the café? It wouldn't be quiet, but I could hide in the back and bake. I wasn't an expert, but I held my own in a kitchen. I helped Sam when he was short-staffed, and I knew how not to get in his way. If all I did today was cook for my friend and his staff, that was fine by me.

Jack smiled at me. Much more of that, and I would start getting ideas. "Could you show me how you open the door when it gets stuck? And where the doorstopper is?"

"You mean right now?" No one had left the library yet, which meant she was still inside. Jack watched me like he had a direct line to my brain and heard my every thought.

"Well, you have been talking out loud for the past few minutes."

I turned my head so hard toward him I got whiplash.

"What?" I squealed.

"I am sorry. I don't know if it qualifies as eavesdropping, but um, you have been thinking out loud, and I wasn't sure how to tell you."

"Well, Detective, your poker face is definitely on point. Next time, warn this boy, will you? I am not sure either of us would enjoy it if you heard everything I am thinking of, especially about you!"

For a fleeting second, he looked intrigued, then schooled his features and looked at me expectantly. Oh right, showing him. I opened the car door and stepped outside. On the plus side, our exchange had revived me.

The noise of people and passing cars assaulted me the second I was out, so much I almost jumped right back into the truck. But I had to do it. Then I would be free, right?

I walked toward the side entrance and stopped at the bottom of the stairs. Something touched my shoulder and I screamed. This was new, even for me. Never before had I been so jumpy. "Hey, it's only me. I am right here, Thibault. Deep breaths, like we did earlier. Do you practice any meditation, yoga?"

I took a few deep breaths, then told him, "Yoga, yes, through an app and at the center once a week, and Nia classes. It's dancing, incorporating a little yoga, dance moves, and some martial arts moves. I don't have a class here, but I do it on Skype with my mam on Saturdays. She shows me the routines she learned the previous Thursday. Yeah, breathing. Breathing is good, isn't it?" I was rambling. I couldn't help it. This was definitely something I did when I was nervous. His hand, still on my shoulder, started stroking. After a couple seconds and some deep breathing, I walked up the stairs.

I stared at the door like it was my first one. The door was opened against the railing, the knob next to the steps. This was so weird. I knew that door; I had opened and closed it almost every day for the past two years. After the doors in my home, I was best acquainted with this door. So to speak. Don't judge me. It wasn't every day I found a body. Merde. I thought I'd put that part of today in the closet for awful memories at the back of my brain and locked it away. Apparently not.

Trying to relax, I took another deep breath. "Here on the floor, that small black thing is our doorstopper. Wait a second. It should be inside. We kept losing them—wind, kids, animals. It changed from one week to the other. So we started putting it back inside every day. Gwendolyn wouldn't have forgotten this either. She closed yesterday, and there is no way she would be this sloppy."

He was once again taking notes. He stopped and looked at me. "Give me one second, please." A few minutes later, he came back with gloves, a few flags, and thingies. He put one flag next to the doorstopper, then handed me a pair of gloves. Was I supposed to put them on?

"Yes, please." Great. Still thinking out loud, I saw. I put on the gloves, which I hated with a passion. I'd had to use some at school, and I had terrible memories of them. I stared at him, waiting. "Right, sorry. Facing where the door would be, could you please show me how you would open the door, and if it stuck, how you would pull it? How do you place your hands?"

I did as he asked, placing my left hand inches away from the doorway, as if grabbing the doorknob and fake inserting the key. I then turned my hand as if twisting the knob and mimed pulling it open and the door resisting. Lifting my right hand, I fake pulled the door toward me with my hand on the inside.

Jack put his hands on my arms and held me there. "Can you rotate your body towards the door?" I twisted my upper body. Sensing him against my back was enough to rattle me and make me shudder. He was warm, alive, and so good against me. I felt sheltered. "I am sorry. I recognize it's a lot, but we are almost done." Thank heavens he hadn't realized he was the reason for my shudder.

My legs facing the door, I slid toward the stairs. Jack moved around me, placing a little sticker, like the ones you used in a book or notebook for studies and such. Hm, that made sense. It would stick to the door where I would have pulled it.

"That's great, Thibault, thank you. You can drop your hands. We are all finished for now. Give me a temporary phone number. I will call you if we have further questions about what you saw or the library itself."

I pivoted to face him. "Sure, give me your notepad." I wrote my number down for him, then remembered I didn't have my mobile anymore as it was still in the library but had written its number out of habit. I wrote my landline number underneath it and looked up expectantly.

The staring contest started all over again. We never did that. The connection I'd experienced for the past two years hadn't been one-sided. But seeing him look at me full of concern or like he wanted to wrap me in bubble wrap and take care of me made me feel seen. Loved. My imagination was running wild. We barely knew each other. We weren't even friends to begin with.

He cleared his throat. Shit, I hoped I'd said nothing out loud. If I had, he didn't remark on it. "You can go now. Why don't you come by the station tomorrow around twelve? Or do you want to stay put in the car until Charlene arrives?"

"I will go to the café if that's okay? Please let her know if she asks for me. I can't handle being alone right now, but I can't stay here. I will help them however I can. Bake or cook or clean, I don't mind. There are a million jobs to handle in this kind of business. That reality squashed my dream of being a baker. So much to do, so little time. I am rambling, aren't I? Stop talking now, Thibault, before you embarrass yourself. Again."

He placed a finger on my mouth. Under normal circumstances, I would have bitten anyone foolish enough to do so, or at least licked them, depending on my level of annoyance. I let out a sigh and spoke against his finger. "I am shutting up now." My words got me another smile from his full, kissable lips. They looked so plush. I bet kissing him would feel... wonderful. I imagined myself tasting his lips, breathing from them. That was the kind of mouth I could devour.

"Sweetheart, why don't you go to the Miracle Brew now? I have your number, and you can call into the station if you remember anything. Even something that seems silly or insignificant. If I am not there, they will transfer you to me."

"Sure." We both took notice at the same time of his finger still on my mouth.

When a throat cleared behind us, we both jumped apart. It seemed to be one of the themes today. Dead bodies, throat clearings, and both of us somewhat acknowledging our deep connection. "Sorry to, um, interrupt, Jack. We are ready to move the body."

I took a step back, and another, and would have fallen down the stairs if it wasn't for Jack's lightning-fast reflexes.

"I am going to go now. I... er. I will see you tomorrow at the station. Bye, guys."

I turned around, rushing away. When I got to the street, some people tried to stop me. An officer I didn't recognize blocked them before they could say anything. I crossed the street and hurried toward the café. I opened the door more forcefully than intended and felt all eyes on me when it banged against the wall. What a stupid idea. I should have gone through the back.

"Sorry, guys. I forgot my wallet and can't leave Reagan alone for too long." No one needed to know that she was at school and nowhere near the library. Reagan was sixteen and our part-timer; at least it would make sense if I was coming like the devil was chasing me. Kind of. I rushed to the counter. Everyone resumed what they were doing. Louder than usual, I said to the barista, "I think it's in the back or Sam might have found it. Do you mind very much if I check with him?" His only answer was to wave me in. I stepped around the counter and stepped into the corridor behind it.

Even though this hallway was nothing like the one at the library, it still brought me back to what had happened, and I had to stop and lean against the wall to try to recover my breath. I started again and walked to the end. In the middle, to my right, was the kitchen, and a quick glance had shown me Sam was not in it.

I tapped on the door to the office, opened it, and stepped in as soon as I heard, "It's open." Not looking anywhere, I moved to the couch and sat down heavily. Sam sat next to me and asked, "Hey, Thibault, what's wrong, sweetie? Do you need anything? Water? Chocolate? The police?" That man understood me so well, placing chocolate before the police. That also meant I was more of a drama queen than I'd thought.

It made me smile. I peeked at him from the corner of my eye. He looked more concerned than I had ever seen him. "No need to call the police. They are there. God, I am not sure if I am even allowed to talk about anything. But he said nothing to the contrary."

"Who didn't, sweetie?" he demanded.

"Jack." Oops. "Detective Tomlins, I mean. I thought there was another break-in at the library when I arrived and found the door unlocked. I went in anyway, pulled up the station's number on my phone while I made my way to the main room. That's when I saw her."

I stopped. I wasn't trying to be dramatic, but just thinking about it made my skin crawl and my stomach rebel. "Could I have a water, please?"

Sam grabbed one from the mini-fridge he kept behind his desk. He brought it back, asking, "What did you find, sweetie?"

I looked up at him. "You remember that story you told me about the blood this morning? Well, it might be a coincidence or not, but hmm, I think I found the body at the library."

"What? Oh my god. Are you okay, Thibault? Jesus, I can't even imagine." He sat down on the sofa and clutched at his chest. Or maybe he was the dramatic one. Though a dead body was definitely no joke.

"I am okay, I guess. It hasn't set in yet. I zoned out a little waiting for the police and then again sitting in his car. He told me to go, but I didn't want to be home alone. Is it okay if I stay for a while? I can help make some food for lunch for you guys, and just bake or wash or even bus tables. As long as I don't have to talk to people, I don't mind."

I was rambling again. It dawned on me I hadn't even asked

who had been killed. Perhaps they didn't know yet. And they wouldn't tell me, would they? That's how it went in the news. They couldn't name the victim until they'd told the next of kin, and sometimes not at all if they were minors. From the little I had seen, she wasn't a minor, but I hadn't seen her face, and clothes could make a person look younger or older depending on what they wore.

Taking my hand, Sam replied, "Sure, sweetie, anything. But first, why don't you drink your water and try to breathe? Hey, I have my yoga mat here, and I'll see if I can find a spare one. Want to do some yoga with me? We can go out back. We will have more space, and you can lead me." When I didn't answer, he uncapped the bottle and brought it to my lips. That pulled me out of my haze.

I snatched the bottle from his hand. I was frazzled, not injured. And I said, "Let's do it. Could I get something to eat first? I left my coffee and scone at the library."

"Let me grab something for you."

Sam came back with the extra yoga mat and a plate with treats. I munched on a muffin without tasting it. After I finished, we went outside and moved through some easy poses of yoga. Nothing was more relaxing to me. It helped a bit, though I could still see her when I closed my eyes, so I stopped after I almost fell doing my second pose.

The rest of the day sped by in a blur. I simply followed the instructions that Sam and his guys gave me in the kitchen. Cleaned tables. Made lunch for everyone. If you asked me now what I'd made for them, I'd have no clue. Or of what I ate either, for that matter.

Around 1:00 p.m., Charlene came by after having talked to the detectives. She scolded me for not calling her. In all fairness, in my half-dazed state, I hadn't remembered I'd said I would. Or that I couldn't, as I didn't have a phone anymore. I knew I kept my old phone somewhere. A temporary SIM card should hold me until I could get my phone back. She didn't blame me when I explained, and as she told me, she had suspected as much but it had still worried her.

By the time 6:00 p.m. came around and the café closed, I was still there. I couldn't face going home alone. Though the discovery had happened at the library, being alone seemed wrong. I was going to ask Sam if he wouldn't mind coming to my place tonight or if I could crash at his after I fed the beasts. Then the café's phone rang. Sam shouted from the kitchen for me to answer as he was elbow deep in soapy water.

"This is the Miracle Brew. How may I help you?"

"Hey, Thibault. It's me, Jack."

"Hey. What can I do for you, Detective?"

"I tried calling you at home, and when there was no answer, I remembered you said you might go to the Miracle Brew. How about I come pick you up and bring you home? I can make you some food and make sure you are not by yourself tonight."

Puzzled, I looked at the phone. Did he just offer to take me home and stay? Jack? "Hmm, sure. I was not looking forward to going home to an empty house."

"Great. Expect me there in fifteen minutes."

He hung up, and I stared dumbfounded at the phone. "Hey, sweetie, what's up? Who was that?" called out Sam, coming my way.

"Detective Tomlins. He is coming over to pick me up, and apparently he is staying. I think?" I was still puzzled over the entire conversation.

"Under any other circumstances, I would start making jokes. But as I was coming over to tell you the same thing, I won't. It's an excellent idea. You might get to know each other."

I looked at him. "You don't think it's weird, after such events?"

"Are you kidding? It's perfect. I didn't say jump his bones. But getting to know each other at a moment where you are vulnerable and less of a porcupine and he can respond to that vulnerability—why not?"

I shrugged. "We will see how things go, but if they get worse, I blame you."

I wasn't sure this was such a splendid idea, but sure, as long as I wasn't alone, I wouldn't be picky. We finished tidying up in silence, waiting for the detective to arrive.

**6**

---

JACK

**Still Friday - Morning**

"I am going to go now. I... er. I will see you tomorrow at the station. Bye, guys." And like that, he was gone.

When I turned around, Marcus had one eyebrow lifted, smiling at me. What was it with people and their eyebrows today? Was there a contest about who would lift them the best or what?

"Oh, wipe that smile off your face, will you? Before you get the body out, let's walk back inside so you can show me what you guys did so far, and I can take over for John."

"You are no fun, Jack," Marcus replied, doing his best impression of a pout. My best friend, ladies and gentlemen: over six feet tall, 220 pounds of muscle, and playful as a puppy. I would be lost without him, but he didn't know when to stop. It was better to nip it in the bud. I was sure he wouldn't forget what he had seen and would bring it up the first chance he got.

"Does the body of someone we both knew for years inside a library we frequented for almost as many of those years sound fun to you?"

"No, sorry, Jacky. I kind of got carried away. This was just too good not to jump on it." He was also the only person who could ever dream of getting away with calling me Jacky.

"Let's get to work. When this is over, you can rib me all you want."

"Jackpot! Man, you shouldn't have said anything. And I want details. There is a story here. I started sensing it a while ago, but every time I try to talk about it, you clam up. You are usually pretty tight-lipped when it comes to people you are going out with or interested in, but this is next level. And with your solemn word to spill the beans, I am looking forward to the gritty details."

I slapped him on the shoulder and propelled him toward the front room.

"Hey, guys, before you bring the body out, what is the progress so far?" Reginald had been quietly writing notes at a table near the front desk while John was taking pictures of the scene. At first glance, it didn't look like much. The flags were concentrated behind the body on the actual front desk and to the sides. Nevertheless, we needed to dust for prints over a considerable portion of the place.

This was going to take us all day. John would go with the doc to help with body transport, cataloging the clothes of the victim and any evidence on her.

Reginald and John came toward Marcus and me. "The body is ready to go. We photographed the room and started with the evidence. We only need to bring the stretcher in and roll her out. I will start on the autopsy straightaway. Nothing new to add about cause or time of death, other than what I found earlier," relayed Reginald.

John added, "I took photos of everything that was here and flagged. My next step would have been bagging and cataloging, then the print lifting."

"Marcus and I will start there, then. Please place the evidence you recover at the morgue in an extra box, separate from the one we are keeping the pond's evidence in. But store them in the same locker. We will need to sort through all of it tomorrow once we finish collecting everything here. If Joss comes in while we are still out, please add his statement to the duck pond box."

Marcus nodded. "We will need to go back to the pond."

We all looked at the scene for a contemplative second. John and Marcus left for the coroner's van and came back in with the stretcher. With great care, we moved Sally Anne to rest on it and zipped the bag over her. We had never been close, but seeing her like that still pained me. Looking at the faces of the three men with me, I realized I wasn't the only one affected by all this.

"All right, boys, let's get moving and solve this." John and Marcus rolled the stretcher out of the room, closely followed by Reginald.

Marcus stepped back in as the truck and a car left. John must have been driving the patrol car. "Give me your keys. I'll park the truck next to Thibault's car in the parking lot at the back. Might make people believe we are done here and move on."

"Were you able to put her in the van unseen?"

"Yes, I think so. It was at a perfect angle."

I handed him my keys.

"Could you please put a Closed For Maintenance sign on the front door before you get back in? I'll see you in a few." And out the back he went.

With him gone, I peeked through the camera to check if

we needed any other close-ups or if I could start bagging the evidence. Satisfied, I placed the camera back in its case, grabbed bags from the evidence kit next to it, and got working.

Marcus came back in when I was ready to start on the front desk itself. I was careful with some of the objects, as blood had transferred onto them. Mostly drops, but a couple could be prints. If they were, I hoped they would not be smudged. Chances were slim of finding someone through that type of print, but you never knew.

We cataloged as we went. With Marcus here, it went faster. I wrote what each bag contained and where we retrieved the evidence from while he put it in the actual bag and labeled it with the evidence number. We could have bagged, then cataloged, but it made things harder.

We kept going until lunchtime came around, finishing the inventory quicker than expected. Then we dusted for prints. While we were debating where to go for lunch, Charlene rang me, asking if she should come in or not as Thibault never called her back. He hadn't mentioned anything, and in his need to leave, I guess he'd forgotten. A little while later, Charlene called out and I told Marcus to take his lunch break and bring me back something once he finished.

I took out my notebook as Charlene and Marcus greeted each other in the corridor. A few seconds later, she came into view. She was in her early fifties, dark haired, petite and plump, always wearing 1950s-style dresses that suited her well. As she had started at the library just a couple of years before I started school and coming to the library, I knew her well. She was strict but always had a kind word for everyone. If you got on her bad side, you'd better watch out. She wouldn't give too many second chances, but if you behaved, she was the best, making lists of books for people depending on what they liked and disliked.

My love for books came from her and this library. Charlene had made me discover so many worlds over the years. Romance drew me in from an early age, and I'd confided in her how it would be great to have more diversity in that category. She understood what I couldn't bring myself to say out loud. Soon after, LGBTQ books started appearing on the shelves of the romance section.

"Hey, Miss Charlene. How are you doing? Thank you for coming in."

"Hey, Jack. Where is Thibault? He didn't call back like he said he might. What happened? Is he okay?" Her voice was rapid-fire. She looked distressed and slightly disheveled, highly unusual for her.

I moved toward her, and rubbing her shoulder, I said in a soothing voice, or as soothing as I could make it, "Why don't we go to your office? We can sit there and be more comfortable while we talk."

"Sure, boy, let's go to my office. But don't think I didn't notice you didn't answer my questions. Whatever happened, he didn't do it."

I chuckled. No surprise there. This woman would go to bat in an instant for anyone she trusted and loved. And from what I'd heard, she considered Thibault family. He was a kind man, and from what I had seen, he made a great impression on visitors to the library.

We arrived in her office and sat on the small sofa in a corner of the room. It would be more comfortable and less formal than at her desk. I'd had a few heartfelt conversations with her here. I couldn't tell her much, but hopefully she would be able to help on some of the points for the investigation.

"First, Ms. Charlene, let me start by saying Thibault was okay when he left, for lack of a better word. Shaken up, for sure, still not realizing what he had seen. He said he was going to go to the Miracle Brew. I am not sure if he is still there, but he needed to keep busy and hoped by helping Sam and his crew, he might get distracted. Why don't you check on him once our conversation is done?"

She simply looked at me and nodded, then waited for me to continue. She had always conducted our discussions this way. I would have to be careful. She always did the one thing my mother couldn't: make me spill my guts with a simple, gentle smile and understanding silence.

I shook my head, trying to sort out my thoughts and decide where to start. "I have a few questions for you if you don't mind. Thibault told me you and your staff come in and out of the side door. You all have keys for that door, as well as some others, but for the front door, only Thibault and you have a key. Is his information accurate and could you provide me a list of the people with a key?"

She stood up and went to her desk, opened one of her drawers, and pulled out a sheet of paper from one of the folders there. Coming back toward me, she said, "There you go, dear, a list of everyone who possesses a key to the library's side door or front door. You can keep it. I will print another one for myself."

I took the paper from her and placed it on the table in front of me.

"Thank you. Next question, do you have an air conditioner in the library, and what temperature do you leave it at for the nights?"

"There is no thermostat. This place is old and the walls are thick, so we don't need to cool it down. We have some fans for the summer when the heat slips in. We use the furnace for the winters. I have a thermometer to check we don't go down too low and the humidity isn't too high for the books. I can't tell you for sure, but we should be at between sixty-six and seventy-two degrees."

"Great, thank you."

Before I could ask anything else, she jumped in. "So now are you going to tell me who was murdered in my library and why so I can whoop their attacker's butt? What kind of animal murders someone in a library? There is enough murdering happening in the war, spy, and crime books to satisfy bloodthirsty people in this town." A startled chuckle escaped me. She wasn't anything if not direct and to the point. Most of the time.

"I am sorry, Ms. C. You know I can't say anything. Much. So far the only ones who know are people at the station, Thibault, you, and me. Do you know if any of the groups with a key had a gathering last night?"

"Humph, you are no fun, darlin'." She paused. "Not that I know of, no. But then again, some of them folks from the HPS, especially that Dorothy woman or her friend, Sally Anne, sneak in to grab some of the books they don't want the rest of us to know they read. Well, thanks to the camera Thibault installed, now I know all about the disappearing and reappearing of our bodice rippers..."

"A camera? Where? I didn't know you had one. I didn't see any signs for a CCTV."

"After the break-in, someone said we should put a camera up. The mayor's office didn't want an extra expense, and some of our charming councilmen laughed in my face. 'Who would want to steal books?' they guffawed. I spoke to the lawyer for the mayor's office. He said we could install cameras ourselves, as long as we showed it. So we did.

"At the back entrance, there is a small sign near the door saying, 'You're being filmed. CCTV camera in action.' If someone comes in the middle of the night fixing to be ugly and doesn't see the sign, then tough for them. Mostly it's animals or children stealing the doorstoppers. Every now and again, it's holier-than-thou church ladies coming in to grab themselves another naughty book. It's been nothing else. We save it all on a DVD we change every Monday. I can ask Thibault tomorrow to give you the DVD for this week, or I can call him now and ask him to come back."

"Thanks, Ms. C. If you can show me where the screen and DVDs are, then I can have a look and remove it myself."

"Sure, dear, it's in the small office next door."

We left her office and went into the room next door, which held a desk with a monitor and recorder on it, a chair, and a large shelving unit. On the opposite wall was a small couch. There was no window in this room, but dazzling lights illuminated it when we turned them on. It must have been a sizeable storage room before they transformed it. Spotting DVDs with no labels, I picked one and went to the desk. I woke the monitor and clicked to stop the recording and eject the DVD. I placed the fresh one in and left the jacket on the desk. I placed the one from the past week into the other jacket and wrote on the label the dates from Monday to today, then underneath wrote, Weatherboro County Library Evidence—Police Department.

"I'll have someone make a copy for you as we will need to keep this as evidence."

"That's all right, dear. I don't think any of us here will want to see what's on it."

"Let's go back to your office. Can you tell me who closed last night and at what time?"

"Yes, Gwendolyn, and on Thursday, we close around 8:00 p.m. Didn't Thibault tell you?"

I ignored the question. I knew what she was asking, but

this was an active investigation, and I had to suspect everyone, even the ones I didn't want to.

We sat back down in her office. "I am not sure how much Thibault told you earlier when he called. This morning he found a body at the front desk of the library. There were signs someone left the back door unlocked. I can't tell you much more." I lifted a hand before she could interrupt me. "Yes, I can't tell you who it was or what happened, especially as it is rather early in our investigation. We will need to keep the scene active today and tomorrow, so the library will have to stay closed. If you could call George this afternoon or tomorrow, he will give you the phone number of the company we contact to clean up crime scenes when needed. They should be able to come in after we release the scene and fix it for you."

"All right, dear. I won't ask. You know you can talk to me, and I would not repeat what you told me to anyone, right? Thank you for letting me know this much, and I promise not to say a word. Now, do you need me or Thibault for anything else?"

"No, I think that's all for the moment. Oh wait, could you provide me with a key for the side entrance? I'll call you, or Thibault, if I think of something else."

We stood up; she got a key from her desk and handed it to me. I took it, the DVD, and the list of key holders. We then left her office and walked to the side entrance. "One more thing. Where is the camera?" We went outside, and there she pointed at a post a few feet away with what looked like a broken street-lamp on top. Just underneath the lamp was the camera. Very good, indeed. I knew there was light in the parking lot. I hoped that it was bright and that, combined with the quality of the camera, we would be able to see something on the recording.

She left then, saying her goodbyes as she went down the stairs. Marcus came back with food. I had stayed out to wait for him so that I could take in some fresh air. The scents near the front desk weren't the worst I'd had the displeasure to smell by far, but being outside still felt nice. The warmth coming off the streets was pleasant. Some clouds were forming to the east, and I hoped they wouldn't come too close, too fast, or too strong. Around this period in previous years, we'd had a couple of nasty storms come in, and I wasn't looking forward to it starting again.

Once Marcus headed up the stairs, we sat at the top so we wouldn't disturb anything inside. He had gotten me a huge salad and a milkshake from Wendy's. I usually brought my own food to the office, but last night I was lazy, thinking I would make lunch this morning. Then life, or more accurately death, had taken the wheel and driven my day off the road.

While we got caught up, I dug in. I told him about the camera outside and the DVD. "I know he was in shock this morning, but why did Thibault not tell us about the recording?"

"What are you saying, Jack? You think he had anything to do with this? Clearly, the guy didn't know she was here or who it was. I mean, he puked."

"Yes, but what does it prove except that someone got sick at our crime scene, and they were careful to do it away from the body?"

"Really, man, you suspect him?" I looked at Marcus and realized we were both frowning. Me because I didn't want to think of Thibault as someone capable of murder. And Lord only knew why Marcus was frowning. I knew he was friendly with Thibault, definitely more than I was, but I hadn't known he was close to him.

I answered, "Not at first, no. But Charlene was quick to say he didn't do it, and I started thinking, *Why would she say that?*

We have no reason to suspect him, other than he found the body."

After taking a big gulp of my milkshake, I continued. "He never asked who the body was. He installed a camera for the library but omitted saying anything about it to us. Thibault and Sally Anne do not get along. Everyone knows about her bigoted and racists views, and she kept getting in Thibault's face about how he was leading the young generations astray, trying to set him up with women regularly and other nonsense.

"They had very heated arguments overheard by quite a few people over the past two years. He knew how to get in here. For all we know, he came with the body through the front door, unlocked the back door this morning, and acted as if it was open. We won't have a way to prove it, even if the camera shows Gwendolyn closing it last night. His prints will be all over the desk, the door, and the doorstop, and we can't prove when he left them.

"As for the vomit, maybe he brought the body in last night, and when he came in today, he realized what he did, and it made him sick. That or the smell. Hell, it wouldn't be the weirdest thing happening to a criminal at a crime scene. Especially after the fact."

I took a breath. God, I hated my job sometimes, but I needed to look at all the facts.

Thibault was the perfect suspect.

**7**

---

JACK

**Still Friday - Early afternoon**

"Jack." The sharp tone in Marcus's voice made me glance at him. While he'd mulled over what I had said, I'd concentrated on my salad and lost myself in my thoughts. He looked thunderous.

"What?" I barked. Was he really going to fight me on this? He knew I was right. "Let's get back to it. We have loads left to do," I growled.

"Nope. I am going to grab my kit and print the door here. We are almost done with the dusting and lifting of prints in the primary room, so you can finish up on your own. Maybe you will pull your head out of your ass while you're at it." Marcus pushed off the stairs and left to retrieve his kit in the front.

When he came back, I asked, "What the berries is wrong with you? You would think I accused your mama of murder."

He shook his head and replied, "Well, you are jumping to the most obvious conclusion before we have even looked at any of the actual evidence, like the DVD on the table inside. You know what I think? If I killed someone and didn't want the attention to turn to me, who would be the perfect fall guy but a transplant who argued with the victim many times? What is the first thing they teach us at the academy? Hell, what is the one thing you always repeat to everyone, even people who have been doing this job for years? 'Review all the evidence with a fine-tooth comb before we draw any conclusions.' Evidence usually leads us to the truth, and more often than not, the guilty party is not who we thought of in the first place. So why are you not following your own advice?

"Because this guy spooks you. I am pretty sure deep down you know he didn't do it, but you can't see past whatever this is, so you have an excuse, once again, to not get close to him. Hell, he just found a dead body. This would be the right time to be there for him, even start a simple friendship with the man. Everyone in town can see what is right under both your noses, but between your stubbornness and his fear of getting rejected or punched in the face, neither of you has the balls to go for it. So let's do this like the professionals we both are, collect the fucking evidence, go through it, and see where it leads us."

He moved to the door, turning his back on me.

I walked back to the information desk for a quick glance at what was left to do and to finish dusting for prints. Funnily enough, there weren't many on the desk, which went with Marcus's theory. Thibault's prints would already have been on the desk and excusable as he worked there every day. Unless he wanted to throw us off.

I cataloged every print we took and placed them into a pile near the evidence, then left for my truck and collected two folded evidence boxes. Once inside, I built them and placed within them all the evidence we'd gathered today, including the DVD and the list of people possessing a key.

Mary, our lab tech, was a whiz when it came to videos. I hoped whatever was on the DVD would give us some indication of the height, size, or gender of our suspect, the exact time, and if they had gone through the side door.

I checked the employee lounge. Apart from the table still holding the scone and coffee, nothing looked out of place in this room. We hadn't checked it yet, everyone going with the assumption that whoever did this had only passed through. I didn't see any blood on the floor, and the body had been dripping blood when it was transported from the pond to their transport vehicle.

Hoping the same thing had happened here and they had wiped it clean, I switched off the lights and asked Marcus to close the door, then switched on my black light. Marcus moved into the room. I took the luminol out. Then, using the black light and with Marcus holding the camera, I went from the door slowly toward the primary room, spraying in front of the door first, then in front of me. About three feet from the door, our first blood drop appeared as a little smear. And there it was: part of a shoe print. Different from the one at the pond, at first glance. Marcus took a picture. As we moved forward, no more prints or blood appeared for a few feet.

But further down, we hit the jackpot. This one was from a right shoe and differed from the first one. Marcus took a few pictures, then ran back out. Once he placed the shoe size marker next to the print, I sprayed again, concentrating the light on it. Shoe size ten. He took a picture. We got a couple more partial shoe prints and blood drops.

We switched the lights back on. "Do you still need time on the door? We should do the railing on the stairs." I looked at Marcus.

"Already taken care of. I was going to come in and ask if you needed help with your part."

The thing was, even though we were still mad at each other, we couldn't go long without talking. First off, because it wouldn't be professional, and second, because we could never not talk to each other. No matter how angry we got, minutes would barely pass before we broke our silence. We would leave the sore subject alone for a while and revisit it later, around beers and some food. Well, when we were kids, it was usually cookies and milk, but we had upgraded over the years.

"I am done as well. Let's pack it up and go back," I told him.

Once we were set, we drove back to the precinct and locked everything away. As we exited the supply room after restocking our kits, the chief appeared in the doorway.

"I need to see you two, now."

We followed him, looking at each other in confusion when we noticed we were going to the conference room. John and Reginald were already waiting, which made sense and explained why we were not in the chief's office.

Once seated, the chief started. "All right, everyone, I need a quick rundown of where you are at so far. News of this has already reached the mayor, and let's just say he would like a swift resolution and arrest."

Seeing everyone looking back at me, I decided to go first, explaining about the scene at the duck pond and what Thibault found at the library. Reginald talked next, explaining his findings.

"Time of death is closer to 8:00 or 9:00 p.m. than 1:00 a.m., as previously suggested. I would say she was kept somewhere else between time of death and being dropped at the library. There was no trace of sexual assault, and the wound to her neck is definitely cause of death. The angle shows it could be accidental more than intentional. And it was definitely someone taller than Sally Anne. We found some trace residues under her nails. I will have my report ready before the end of the day."

The chief nodded. "Great. Now, do we have any suspects or evidence which can narrow down who it could be?"

I prepared to speak, but Marcus cut me off. "Not really so far. We have shoe prints and fingerprints, so hopefully something will come of that. Our best hope is a video from the camera installed outside the library."

"What are your next steps then, Detectives? We need something fast," the chief said.

I looked at Marcus and nodded at him to continue.

"We need to check, but as far as I know, Dorothy is our next target. Sally Anne was divorced, and I think her next of kin is living in a different state, so if anyone has a spare key and would know of any enemies or problems Sally Anne might have had, it would be Dorothy. Someone should go back to the duck pond, see if they can find her car, wallet, phone—anything that might help."

The chief nodded. "Jack, do you have anything to add?" I shook my head. I didn't want to speak. I didn't know what else to say, except point out how Thibault might be our suspect. I wasn't sure why Marcus had elected to not talk about him to the chief.

"All right, well then. John, please grab anyone who is free and go check out the duck pond. See if you can find anything. Jack, Marcus, go see Dorothy. See if she can help and then go secure Sally Anne's home. Let George know who next of kin is so he can contact them."

We all nodded and left the room. We told George what he needed and let him know we would call or text once we were at Dorothy's. He provided us with her address.

Following John outside, we took the car and drove to

Dorothy's home. She was living near Robertson Boulevard, south of town on a quiet street. Her home was a classic two-story white house. Pretty, with a well-tended front garden and a large tree shading the entrance.

Once at her front door, we hesitated. Telling someone one of their loved ones had passed away was always difficult. Sally Anne's gruesome death would make things harder to digest. I braced myself as Marcus rang the doorbell.

It took a few seconds before the door opened. Seeing us there, Dorothy's first word was "No."

"Dorothy. Could we come in?"

She shook her head, but then stepped out of the way and gestured for us to follow. She sat heavily on a chair in what looked to be her sitting room.

"Would you like some tea or coffee?" she asked.

"No, thank you," Marcus answered while I shook my head in the negative.

Marcus gestured for me to talk.

I swallowed hard. "Dorothy. By the way you reacted at seeing us, I guessed you might have an idea why we are here. Sally Anne's body was found this morning. By what the coroner has learned so far, it appears she was murdered." I paused then, thinking carefully over what to say next.

At my announcement, Dorothy uttered another shocked "No" and started crying.

"We are really sorry for your loss," Marcus added. Crap. I usually let him talk to victims or loved ones of victims for a reason. I wasn't heartless, like a widow had accused me of being once. I was so focused on the investigation and how I could find justice for the victims, I sometimes forgot the living and breathing people I was addressing.

"What do you want, Detectives? Who found the body?" she choked.

I ignored the second question, answering only the first. "There was no handbag found at the crime scene. As you two have always seemed close, we were hoping you had a key to her place and if you could give it to us? We would need her phone number as well."

"I do. Let me find it for you."

Crying silently, she left us then, walking out of the room. She came back a couple of minutes later, a key in her hand and a determined look on her face.

"Here is the key." She started handing it over, but as Marcus grabbed for it, she moved back, her eyes narrowing. "Who found her?" she snapped.

"Thibault Abrams was opening the library this morning when he discovered her."

She shouted, "That bastard!" Shaking her finger in both our directions, she exploded. "You better have arrested that man. My poor Sally Anne. He murdered her. He assaulted her yesterday. The fight must have continued."

"Assaulted?" I asked, pulling out my notebook while Marcus tried to placate her and make her sit down at least. He sat back next to me, putting the key into an evidence bag, then quickly into his pocket, as if afraid Dorothy might snatch it back.

"She heard him talking to someone about the perversion he was getting up to with a man. She told him off, and he told her she would regret this," she offered, sounding somewhat calmer. Before screeching, "He must have killed her for telling the truth in front of everyone!"

Biting his lip and frowning, Marcus shook his head slightly while taking notes in his pad.

"Thank you, Dorothy. That was definitely something I wasn't aware of," I answered. "We need to go to Sally Anne's home now. We will call you if we have any further questions."

She nodded, reclining in her chair, defeated and deflated.

"Thank you for your time. I am really sorry for your loss," I added.

She waved me off. I made my way outside as Marcus asked if she had anyone to come and stay with her for the night. Already at the front door by then, I didn't hear her reply.

We walked back to the car. Once inside, I turned to Marcus. "Care to tell me why you were shaking your head so hard at her when she said Thibault killed Sally Anne over a fight they had? Did you know? How? Why didn't you tell me? What else are you omitting?"

"Nothing, Jack. Come on, don't give me that look. I was at the Miracle Brew when the fight started. Sally Anne told Thibault he was a pervert, as usual. She raved about something she overheard and he apparently made up. She told him he would burn in hell and 'pay for his sins.' He never once threatened her or did anything other than talk back and defend himself."

"So, the usual then. But it still goes with my theory."

"Couldn't help yourself, could you? I am telling you he didn't do it. Fight or not, what motive would he have? Since he arrived in town two years ago, she has been on his back. Dorothy as well. Always picking fights with him because unlike most of us, he fought back." He scoffed. "You really think that was the first time some bigot told him something like that? Hell, in that case, I would have killed a lot of people. Between my being black and bisexual, the bigots and the racists have plenty of reasons to pick fights."

His words gave me pause. But I couldn't shake the idea of Thibault having something to do with this. Whether it was instinct, intuition, or like Marcus pointed out, my need to find more excuses to put Thibault at a distance, I didn't know and I didn't want to look at it too closely.

We spent the rest of the drive to Sally Anne's house in silence. As it was a brief journey, it went fast, which I was thankful for. Once there, we rang the bell. I am not sure what either of us expected to happen. There was a car in the driveway, which could have been what had confused us.

After a minute, I looked at Marcus, raising an eyebrow. "As you are the one with the key, would you mind opening the door?"

He looked at me in surprise, then pulled out the key. "Sorry, I forgot. This all feels surreal."

"I know what you mean. I never thought one of us would ever go into Sally Anne's home uninvited."

"Well, I don't think we should ever expect these kinds of things. It would make life too miserable and hard to live."

I nodded. I completely agreed. Dealing with death and the horrors you were confronted with as a cop was hard. That was one of the reasons why I'd requested a transfer a few years ago from Charleston back to Weatherboro. The happenings in a big city had taken their toll on me. My first year in Columbia had been the worst. Working for a medium-sized town felt right and didn't come with the same heartaches as the bigger cities. However, things were getting a little more grueling because the town was growing.

Once inside, the quiet was almost oppressive. We went through the different rooms, checking no one was in them and everything was where it should be. Once we made our rounds, I noticed two things. Her laptop was right on the kitchen table, as if waiting for her to come back, and there were dog dishes but no traces of a dog.

We checked and bagged everything relevant to us. Before we left, I put a seal on her front and back doors.

Had the dog died? Did it live with the ex-husband? Or was

it with one of her friends? But that would be weird. We would have to ask Dorothy.

We went back to the precinct. After placing everything away into the evidence locker, we tried switching on her laptop. It was password protected. Marcus connected a little device he got from Mary to figure out the password and allow us access. It would take a while, so we plugged it in and left it there.

On the way back to our desks, I noticed Mary was hard at work on something.

I popped my head in. "Hey, Mary. How are you doing, lady? Find anything interesting already?"

"Hey, Jack. No, not yet. You know how it is—it will take me a while."

"No worries. Let us know as soon as you get something. Especially from that video."

"Will do, Jack. Have a good night."

Surprised, I looked at my watch. I noticed it was almost 6:00 p.m.

I went back to my desk and noticed Marcus wasn't there. I called John quickly.

"Hey, John, it's Jack. Any luck?"

"Hey, Jack. I walked out on both sides. No sign of anything. I encountered someone on the way back, and they notified me of a dead buck further up, but apart from that, nothing else. No body, no purse or personal belongings. I checked the dumpsters along the way. I am turning back now and almost at the duck pond, but the rain is closing in. I will detour by the library on my way to the station. While I was checking the dumpsters here, I realized none of us checked the ones at the library. Or did you and just didn't mention it?"

Well hell, no, we hadn't. That's why multiple pairs of eyes, brains, and hands were useful in such cases.

"You're right. Not sure how we missed something so basic. Thanks, John, excellent catch."

"No problem. Talk to you tomorrow. Have a good night."

I went in search of Marcus and found him at the entrance with George. "Hey, folks. John is on his way back. No luck at the duck pond. He will stop at the library and look for the purse in the dumpsters, as we forgot to."

Marcus nodded. "Great, I was just thinking about where to find that purse. We need her phone. I am hoping we might get something out of it."

George nodded and added, "I was able to reach Sally Anne's niece. She didn't seem too happy at the idea of coming here for her aunt, but she should be able to fly in within the next two days. I notified her ex-husband as well, as per the chief's request. He almost hung up on me."

Mary came around the corner. "You still here, Jack? You look like you haven't slept in three days. You're getting old, my friend, if waking up at five is making you seem half dead."

I snorted, "Thanks, lady, not sure my ego will recover from that one." They all looked at me like I had sprouted a rainbow horn. Yeah, I was definitely not the most playful man out there.

They smiled at me. "I will get out of your hair real quick." Patting myself, I realized I'd left my phone at my desk. I went back, grabbed my things, and was going to leave when I remembered I wanted to see someone. I still felt conflicted about what the evidence pointed to, but I needed to be with Thibault tonight. I stepped back to my desk and called the number on my notepad. It rang and rang. After a minute, I hung up. I looked up a certain coffee store's number online, then dialed it instead.

"This is the Miracle Brew. How may I help you?" Hearing his voice felt nice. I didn't want to think too hard about how easily I recognized it. I was happy and, weirdly enough, relieved he was still there. If I could give him a ride home, it would feel less like I was crowding him.

"Hey, Thibault. It's me, Jack."

"Hey. What can I do for you, Detective?"

"I tried calling you at home, and when there was no answer, I remembered you said you might go to the Miracle Brew. How about I come pick you up and bring you home? I can make you some food and make sure you are not by yourself tonight."

"Hmm, sure. I was not looking forward to going home to an empty house."

"Great. Expect me there in fifteen minutes."

I left the bullpen and sped to the front door. The smile on my face got me another round of weird looks. "Night, guys. See you bright and shiny in the morning." Okay, that was pushing it too far to the opposite side of grumpy. And there went Marcus's eyebrow. Well. I knew the circumstances were not ideal, and if I told my best friend where I was going, I would receive another (deserved) lecture.

I made my way outside, and seeing how close the rain was already, I took the car. Thibault might not be in a state to drive, and it would be easier for me to get back in the morning and let him sleep in. That gave me the opportunity right now to drive home, get changed into something more comfortable, and grab some clothes and toiletries for the morning before picking him up.

I was at the coffee shop within twenty minutes. When I arrived, the door was locked. Thibault and Sam were finishing the cleanup inside. I tapped on the window frame, careful not to smear the glass.

Thibault opened the door for me. "Hey, Detective, come on in. How are you? Long day, huh? I am sure you just want to go home and stay off your feet. I can go alone—it's fine. I am fine. Never felt better. You know. No big deal. I'll go shopping. I forgot yesterday and the day before, and the one before that. So I am going to go now. And then I'll go pick up my car. Or, wait, I should pick up the car first, then go shopping. Oui, oui, it does make a lot more sense de toute façon."

He stopped abruptly. He'd either realized he was rambling or that he had spoken in French. He grimaced and his head snapped in Sam's direction, and I realized it was neither. I hadn't thought of option three. "Did you just pinch me?" I tried my hardest not to laugh, but a chuckle escaped me all the same. They both turned and stared at me. Did I laugh or smile so little it seemed surprising to people?

I shook my head. "Like I said on the phone, Thibault, I don't mind. We can go to the shops close to here or to Walmart if you need a lot of things. It will go faster with the two of us, and you can help me chose what to cook for you tonight."

"Well, no, Detective."

I interrupted him. "Jack, please."

"Sure, Jack. As I was going to say, if you insist on coming with me, then the least I can do is cook for you. I have dessert already, and I can whip up something simple and easy."

I tried not to interpret his words the way I wanted them to sound. This wasn't a date.

"Let's go. It will start to rain soon, and it would be best if we don't get caught up in it. I have the truck. I'll give you a lift to your car tomorrow. Goodnight, Sam."

Sam waved at me and gave Thibault a kiss on the cheek, all the while pushing him toward the door.

Thibault grumbled. "All right, all right, I am going. Stop it, you pushy man. I'll see you tomorrow, love."

# 8

JACK

**Still Friday - Evening**

When we exited, the wind had picked up, and we jumped into the truck. I drove us to the grocery store. Shopping with this man was weird. It felt almost domestic, especially when we started arguing about what was best, fresh or bagged salad. I liked fresh but I sometimes preferred mixed bags, as you could get a variety of salads in one go. He argued for fresh salad, then ended the entire conversation by saying, "I grow my own salad, so it's a moo point."

"You mean moot point."

"Nope," he popped out with a smirk. Well, at least our salad argument had brought back his sassy side.

Wait a second. "What do you mean you grow your own salad? You started this." He shrugged again. God, my need to strangle him would one day get the better of me.

"Thibault," I growled, in what I thought was a menacing voice, especially when I saw him shudder.

"God, Detective, that voice. Trying to turn me on in front of the tomatoes and half the town? You making sure I am not the only blushing and traumatized person here today?" Well, I stood corrected. I elicited a shiver. Good to know. And he had turned me around, again. He would drive me to distraction faster than to homicide.

"Moving on. I know English is mixed up for you, but it is definitely a moot point and not moo."

"How disappointing, Detective. I thought an older man like you would know his classics. Let me give you a clue—my friends Joey and Rachel."

And that's when it hit me: he was quoting *Friends*. I was more tired than I'd thought if the reference had slipped past me, especially something I quoted often enough myself.

"Touché, little man." Apparently, if there was one thing he hated more than Mister Abrams, it was being called *little*. His gaze went wide, then narrowed almost as fast. He started forward again, bypassing most of the vegetables and fruits, only grabbing some early, delicious-looking strawberries.

"Sorry, little man. I know you're the one cooking tonight, but I am going to need more vitamins and protein." I felt myself blush as I realized what had just come out of my mouth. It wasn't as visible on me as on him, but it was there.

He quirked an eyebrow at me, then quipped, "No worries, Detective. I have all the protein and vitamins you could ever need at home." And that's when I squeaked and choked on air. His laugh was bright and charming, if a little softer and more subdued than usual. "Get your mind out of the gutter, Jack." God, the way he made my name sound was almost enough to make me grow hard in my jeans. The fact that he'd never used my name before today was an excellent thing. I didn't need this kind of reaction in public.

"I grow my own vegetables. I enjoyed it back in Ireland with my parents, though the climate wasn't always the easiest on our most delicate plants. I have to say I prefer it here. The weather is brilliant for the fruits in particular. My mam always loved homemade jams, and I am happy to make such a great variety now, thanks to Ruth's bushes."

I nodded. "I am glad to hear it. We had to plant extras when some of the older ones died. It was a painful process, especially the thorny ones, but so rewarding." He looked shocked for a second, and I could see the questions dancing in his mind, ready to tumble forward. Bracing myself for the avalanche, I felt a hand on my shoulder with a delicate clearing of a throat. I registered the scowl on Thibault's face and almost didn't turn.

My mama drilled all sorts of respectful manners and behavior into me from a young age, and I never could shake them. Even after I left home at eighteen, I never swore. The only thing I had always done, as my own personal rebellion, was take the good Lord's name in vain. It had irritated her to no end to my great pleasure. Thibault's signals or not, I was compelled to move and face whoever it was. When I did, I wish I hadn't.

Jessica looked at me, a hopeful and friendly smile on her face. My first thought was, Not now. Every time we met went the same way.

We had known each other most of our lives. And it was one of those classic things that wouldn't go amiss in a rom-com. The predictable ones. While I'd played any sport I could, she was head cheerleader and on different school committees. She made her interest known early on, and people tried to put us in each other's path. I had always kept to myself. I flirted with girls, just to fit in, but never with her. I'd suspected she wouldn't have let it go.

I was right. Even with no encouragement on my part, she never let the marvelous romance idea drop. I think she set her mind on me as we started junior high, and encouraged by her mama and my own mother, she started pursuing me our senior year. I had tried to let her down gently, but it didn't work. And after all these years and one of her friends outing me, she still thought she had a chance. My mother kept encouraging her, throwing fuel on the fire, because only a respectable woman would bring me into the fold. Pah.

Yeah, no. This would never happen. She wasn't a man. More to the point, she wasn't Thibault. The man who could be everything I wanted. No, scratch that—he was everything, no could about it. If only I would let myself open up to him.

They were opposites in looks. Where she was tall for a woman, he was small for a man, and she had at least an inch on his five-foot-seven-inch frame. She had curves in all the right places on a slender body, where he was in shape with a little belly. He had long dark (sometimes) curly hair; she had a short blond bob. She had big blue eyes set in a heart-shaped face, where his features were sharp with intelligent hazel eyes I enjoyed getting lost in. He had a sprinkle of stubble; she didn't, that I could see. The only thing they had in common, I guess, was the touch of makeup they both wore, and even there they didn't match. Their sense of style was different too, except today where they both wore business casual.

I was so lost in my comparison I startled when she spoke.

"Hey, Jack. How are you doing? Long time no see."

"I am good, Jessica. I hope you are doing fine as well?"

"Yes, thanks. I wanted to talk to you. How about getting a coffee together this week? Your mother told me she was going to see you and would remind you to call me, but she must have forgotten."

Wonderful. My mother was back to her old tricks. I had barely listened to her voicemail. Once I realized nothing was wrong with her or Father, I deleted it, especially when she started talking about the next event they were going to and how I needed to be there and she had a suitable date for me. I hadn't gone for years now. If I went anywhere my parents might be, I usually brought Marcus or Bobby with me and stuck to them like glue, avoiding my parents at all costs. But every few weeks, she tried anyway. I hadn't talked to my mother in six months. It always went the same way, and apart from leaving me exhausted and sad, it changed nothing.

"I am sorry, Jessica, but whatever event my mother promised I would attend with you, I won't be able to make it. And I will be extremely busy over the next few days at the station. Now, if you would excuse me, I have to get back to Thibault. We need to finish grocery shopping and get him home." I was rude and, depending on how she interpreted my words, very misleading.

"Oh, yes, I heard he had quite the shock this morning. How dreadful. It is so good of you to take care of him, Jack. The poor thing has no one here, from what I was told. He needs a woman in his life to take care of him. Why don't you call me this week as soon as you are free for that coffee, and I'll see if I can find him a date? Oh, we could all go out together. It would be wonderful."

I heard a snort behind me. Just as I opened my mouth to retort, she said, "Don't let me keep you. Have a nice evening." She turned on her heels and walked into a different aisle.

Behind me, Tom had joined Thibault. He was an amiable man in his mid-forties, about five feet eleven inches, with thinning dirty blond hair and a nice build. He owned one of the garages in town. He and Thibault were friendly. When Tom had taken over from his father, the shop was failing. Thibault, as part of the initiatives he'd put in place at the library, helped promote his business, and it was now doing much better.

They both were looking at me, Thibault frowning and Tom smiling.

"Hey, Detective, how are you doing?"

"I am fine, thanks. Could one of you tell me how she could have interpreted what I said as me agreeing to call her for coffee?" I asked.

Thibault shrugged, turned around, and moved away.

Puzzled, Tom looked at him go and turned back to me, saying, "Well, I never have the best of luck with the ladies, so I wouldn't know for sure, Jack, but maybe you should give her a chance. You are not getting any younger and..." He stopped mid-sentence and took a step back. My scowl must have returned in full, but I couldn't help it.

"And?" I inquired.

He swallowed.

"Oh, come on, Jack, give it a rest. Your mother has been telling everyone for years that what that Mandy girl revealed at your graduation was just poppycock, as her son could not have 'chosen' to live in sin. She has been denying your sexuality for the past fifteen years and telling anyone who would listen you and Jessica will get married any minute now."

I turned around toward the voice of none other than our previous chief, Anthony Allen.

"Sir, it's good to see you. I am sorry, Tom. I didn't mean to scowl. It has just been a trying day."

Tom looked at me, sheepish. "No, I am the one who is sorry, Jack. I should have known better. I see your father and Jessica's father on and off at the shop, and they keep talking about how you two are so close and just haven't decided on a wedding date. I know you are, well, not interested in women, but hearing them talk, it sounded like a done deal. Your dad keeps saying you being gay was only a phase and the police cured you of this nonsense. His words, not mine. But I shouldn't have listened or assumed." And I understood, even if it hurt me every time I heard about it.

"Well, what a load of horseshit," said Chief Allen. "As if you could turn it on and off. I keep telling my son he can rant at me and his daughter all he wants about god and whatnot. My girl was born this way, and she won't change her mind about liking girls simply because her daddy said so. You should know better, Tom. Now, son, how is the investigation going?"

I couldn't help but smile. This man had been an outstanding grandfather figure to me since I was small, then became a great mentor and a wonderful friend. "Ah, now, Chief, you should know better than to ask."

Tom looked curious. "Is it true that someone found a body at the library and it was murder?"

"I am sorry, Tom. It goes for both of you. I cannot mention anything about what happened today. George notified next of kin, but that is all I am able and willing to say."

"Is it true it was Sally Anne?"

Something crashed to the floor, and I saw Thibault staring at us, wild-eyed. Poppy seeds. "I am sorry, gentlemen. I need to go. I wish you both a great evening."

Once I reached Thibault, he was looking at me like he had seen a ghost. "Sally Anne?" he whispered.

"Hey, sweetheart, take a deep breath, please. Here is what we will do. First, we finish shopping for what you have on your list. Then we will cook and talk, all right? Can you do that for me?" I whispered back.

He looked at the floor and nodded. Then he squared his shoulders, left me with the shopping cart, and hunted for something to clean the floor with. Tom and Anthony were looking at us with very interested expressions, but they scattered off when they noticed me.

As soon as Thibault was back, we finished his shopping.

Once he paid at the cashier, we made our way outside. The wind was even stronger now, and fat drops of rain were falling. The smell of warm earth and fresh rain started coming up.

"That's one of my favorite smells," said a small voice beside me. I looked at Thibault as he continued. "It doesn't smell the same at home, but I just love it, that first drop of rain on the hard earth, baked all day in the sun. It always soothes me."

"Yeah," I whispered back. Then louder, "We should go before we get soaked loading everything in the car."

We made fast work of the groceries, then started for his place. Having taken the road so many times over the years, I knew it by heart. First as a child with my family, my nanny, or the bus to school. As a teenager with my beat-up truck. And until two years ago, I went every weekend to keep an eye on Ruth and help with the animals.

We arrived at the farmhouse faster than I'd wanted to. I hadn't stepped foot here in two years. This was going to bring back so many memories for me. I dreaded it as much as I looked forward to it. Thibault sat there staring too, but his thoughts were not on the same page as mine. For now I needed to put aside my own feelings. I could go down memory lane once we were both in bed.

I gently touched his shoulder. "Let's get everything inside and start cooking." We unloaded it all in one go and went in as the rain started coming in faster. Shaking off the dampness, we moved to the kitchen. I was happy to see he'd kept things the same way Ruth had. Apart from a fresh coat of paint, the entrance and the kitchen looked the same to me.

The corridor wasn't large, but it had enough space for a coatrack, a new shoe stand, and a pretty commode where Ruth used to keep all sorts of things. The walls were now a warm light gold, and the black wood of the cabinet contrasted nicely. On it were a couple of vases I remembered being in the sitting room before, as well as a lovely knitted doily on which sat a large, flat glassware pot. Thibault threw his wallet and keys inside with some letters on the way to the kitchen. To the left of the entrance sat the living room and opposite was the sitting room. At the end of the corridor, straight on, sat the kitchen, and right before it was the staircase for the second floor's bedrooms and bathrooms. Nestled under the stairs was a small half bath, and opposite was the laundry room.

The kitchen was now a soft shade of orange, like a ripe peach, and he'd repainted the cabinets in a dark gray. He'd kept the same ones but removed the doors for some and replaced others with glass and intricate woodwork. The pantry had stayed the same. The appliances were new, though, a mix of dark and light colors. A blend of her personality and the history of the house, with his own touch shining through.

While I was in the pantry, the back door opened, followed by a quiet woof and displeased meows. I moved back into the kitchen to find five pairs of eyes facing me, a wide-open door, and no Thibault. I rushed to the stairs leading to the back garden, remembering at the last second to switch on the floodlights. I didn't notice him at first and meant to close the door, but a light shone in the distance. After a few minutes, he emerged from the barn. Despite getting soaked, he picked vegetables and placed them into a wicker basket. Daylight was fading fast. With the rain, I was happy for the light as it let me see him more clearly in the storm's darkness.

"What are you doing?" I half shouted over the wind.

He looked up. "The animals needed feeding. And I promised you dinner. Can't do that without getting my ingredients." He ran into a vast greenhouse, definitely not here two years ago. A few minutes later, he came back out, closed the door, and ran toward me. He shoved me inside and closed the door behind us.

"That wasn't necessary. I wouldn't have died from having pasta for one night or whatever else you might have here that wouldn't involve you getting sick."

Pushing past me, he put his basket on the kitchen table. He stepped out of his shoes and removed his clothes right there, stripping down to nothing. His hands hovered above his underwear, but he seemed to think better of it. God, seeing his body was enough to ignite mine with want. He was lean, with the outline of muscles in his arms and legs. I hadn't expected that. When we usually collided, his body always felt soft and supple in my arms. Except on the one occasion seared in my memory. But I'd always thought his force then was more thanks to adrenaline and taking me by surprise than actual strength.

For the past two years, I had been curious to know what was underneath the clothes, especially after Pride. It had been too dark that night for me to see much of anything. Now I knew. I took in his pale skin, the curve of his butt, and I wanted to run my hands slowly all over that deliciousness. I swallowed thickly. It must have been louder in the kitchen's silence than I imagined, as his gaze found mine. He winked, picked up his clothes, and headed to the laundry room right off the kitchen. He started the dryer and left.

Now I was alone with his cats, dogs, and fresh vegetables. The cat and dog food was in the same place, so I took the liberty of feeding them. They looked happy and content. I picked the fresh produce out of its basket. Radish, salad leaves, small cucumbers, and tomatoes.

As I washed the vegetables, Thibault came back in wearing loose pants and a dark gray sweater that looked soft and fit his frame well. He smiled at me. In this kitchen, with the small dimple to the side of his left lip, he reminded me so much of Ruth. She used to smile at me the same way in this very room.

He pulled out two cutting boards, pasta, a salad bowl, ham, and knives. While the pasta cooked, we got working on the rest. I noticed how he diced his vegetables and tried to do the same. Soon enough, the bowl was full, and we added the ham and the pasta. He made a sauce and set it aside. Being around him felt nice, very homey. I shouldn't get used to it, but it was so comfortable.

I kept stealing glances. He appeared so young and vulnerable, with an added air of confidence, doing something he was good at. His black hair was still wet from the rain and curling around his shoulders. In this light, his features seemed sharper than usual. A straight nose, almond eyes, and a bow-shaped mouth, sharp cheekbones that would get a splatter of freckles in the summer. He was gorgeous. And it made me aware that we had a difference of almost a foot in height, so I felt gigantic next to him.

Every time he stepped close to me to drop things in the bowl, I felt his body heat and I got a little distracted, thankfully not enough to cut a finger. That would have been quite the end to our already fun day.

We grabbed plates, sat down at the kitchen table, and started eating. The silence grated. I didn't mind quiet, but around people, especially at this kitchen table, bringing back so many memories, it was unbearable. As I racked my brain to find a safe enough topic to talk about, Thibault spoke.

**9**

---

THIBAULT

**Still Friday - Evening**

"*I* am sorry," I breathed. "I shouldn't have done that earlier, Jack."

"What are you sorry for? I enjoyed feeding the animals. Or do you mean for running around in the rain?"

Though his blush told me he knew exactly what I was talking about, he was either trying to deflect or hadn't see me naked.

"Neither. Thanks for feeding the animals. As for the rain, I am used to it. I mean, Ireland is not as wet as everyone makes it sound, but it does rain quite a bit. You can't stop doing things simply for the fear of catching a chill, my mam always told me." I took a sip of water. "I meant more the getting naked in the middle of the kitchen. I won't say I forgot you were there, but I just needed to get out of my clothes. As I live alone, that's what I usually end up doing."

"Nothing to be sorry about. I definitely didn't mind." He sounded as surprised by his words as I was. The flush burning my cheeks and neck was reflected, to a lesser extent, on his face. Huh. I'd never caught that before. Or at least I'd never watched him closely enough before to notice his blush. Jack's face almost glowed in the warm light of the kitchen, the blush softening his features. The wind had mussed his dirty blond hair, and I wished my hands had been responsible. His full kissable lips were surrounded by a well-trimmed blond-and-silver beard, and his hooded green eyes sparkled in the light.

Clearing my throat, I blurted out the one question dancing in my mind since we'd left the store. "Was it Sally Anne at the library?"

His sigh was heavy. He didn't seem to know how to answer. But if they'd contacted the next of kin, then they were aware of who it was, and they could talk about it, couldn't they? I needed to know who I'd discovered. It wouldn't help me sleep better or bring them back, but at least they wouldn't be a faceless corpse in my head anymore.

Finally, he said, "Yes, it was. I can't tell you anything else, Thibault, but I am pretty sure this particular piece of information is already running through town at the speed of light."

We both fell silent again and finished eating. Mon Dieu, poor Sally Anne. Don't get me wrong. I held no love for that spiteful woman, but no one deserved to be hurt or killed and left somewhere for someone else to find. Who did that kind of thing? I mean, on TV and in movies, sure, but in real life? Deep down, I knew it happened. It didn't shock me any less. I had seen it during my time in college, as I'd minored in criminology, but I never would have expected it to befall someone I knew.

We brought the dishes to the sink, and I started cleaning them, adrift in my thoughts. Seeming lost too, Jack dried and put things away once I placed them on the drying rack. The sadness in his eyes surprised me. What thoughts ran through his head to bring such an expression to his face?

Once finished, I turned to him. "Would you like something to drink and to watch some TV? I am sure you are tired and I am bone weary, but I need to stop thinking for a little while. Otherwise, I won't be able to sleep."

He smiled faintly. "Sure, I wouldn't mind something warm. I'll go switch on the TV."

"Bailey's hot chocolate with a slice of banana bread?"

"Sounds great, thank you."

I made the drinks, added a good dose of Bailey's to both our glasses, and cut two generous pieces of the bread. I needed some comfort food, and the look in Jack's eyes told me he did too. His lack of protest said a lot. I placed the goodies on a tray and made my way to the sitting room when I realized he'd never asked where he needed to go. Granted, it wasn't that difficult, but still, I would have asked. Same for the kitchen. He had moved around it, putting things in the right place like he had done so a million times.

Even though I'd understood someone had been helping Ruth before she'd passed, I'd never discovered who. Seeing how comfortable Jack appeared here and the sadness in his eyes, I sensed the person was right in front of me.

When I arrived in the sitting room, the TV was off and Jack was staring into space. He had switched on the radio, playing soft rock tunes from one of my favorite stations. I had kept Ruth's delicate antique radio. Overall, I had changed little in the house. She had kept it all in great condition.

I'd repainted everything. The sitting room and dining room now sported light shades of pink and lavender, respectively, fitting well with the black wood furniture that I kept. I'd considered changing things but went against it. I often went with my gut instinct, and here it was telling me the time wasn't right just yet for major changes. If only I had listened to it this morning.

I put everything on the small table in front of the couch Jack sat on. I'd started for the chair next to the couch when I noticed the cats and dogs scattered all around Jack. Sandy, a British Shorthair, had claimed the chair that I had been going for. At her feet was Scout, the Border Collie.

Behind Jack was Smokey, my Himalayan cat. Next to her was Spot, my Scottish Fold. Under the couch, peeking from between Jack's legs, was Skye, the Australian Shepherd. Going through the vet records, I had learned their distinct breeds and kept a list of what each of them needed. I didn't want to mess it up, so I had read a lot on each of them. They were all between three and eight years old, Spot being the youngest.

Finding them all around him was surprising. They were skittish on the best day. They had gotten used to me and were now all over me when I was home. Often enough, they would be in a similar position around me, with one or two using me as their chair. Sandy wasn't going anywhere, so I sat next to Jack. Spot jumped down onto the couch, stretched, and settled on my lap. I looked up to find Jack peering at me. "That's Spot, right? She did the same thing with Ruth but never with me. She was all over Miss Ruthie as soon as she sat down."

"Spot was young when I arrived, and she was the first one to accept me. We were all wary of each other. I didn't have pets as a child as my dad was allergic to them. Or at least so he claims," I said with a smile. "But weirdly enough, at other people's houses or now when they come to visit me here, my dad never has an allergy attack." That made him chuckle. But the haunted look remained in place.

I rubbed his arm while reaching for my hot cocoa. "Jack, talk to me. We know little about each other, but I promise a judgment-free zone. And to be honest, I could use the distraction. That came out wrong. It is not a distraction. Not if it makes you look haunted. But it would keep my brain from wandering to territories best left alone. You know, I can still see her body. And that smell keeps coming back. It's embedded in my nose. I wanted to take a shower earlier but didn't want to leave you alone too long. But now it just..."

He stopped me again with a finger on my mouth. I couldn't help it this time. I licked it. That got me a deep chuckle, a warm smile, and a heated gaze.

"Drink your cocoa, Chatty Cathy, and let me tell you a story." He took a large gulp of his. He must have grabbed the cup while I was rambling. I was either sarcastic or chatting a mile a minute around this man. He coughed. "Whoa, there is quite a dose of Irish in this hot chocolate. Now, where to start?"

"Here is a thought. Why not from, oh, I don't know—the beginning?" I couldn't help myself, could I?

"Thanks. It didn't occur to me," he deadpanned. I wasn't used to that side of him, but I liked what I had seen so far. Throughout the day, we had seen each other in a new light. I hoped, like me, he might want to explore this further. His being here having spiked cocoa on my couch hopefully meant he did.

"I have lived here my whole life. My parent's farm isn't too far, a couple miles down the road. I remember going on bike rides or in the car with my nanny and Marcus. She would bring us here. David and Ruth never had children. They always let Marcus and me in to visit the exotic animals and help feed them. Later on, when we were old enough, they let us muck the stalls, help with the crops, that sort of thing. This became my haven, especially after I turned fourteen and started coming to terms with some things about myself. Ruth sat me down and told me they would always welcome me here, no matter what.

"David died shortly after my graduation. Things had gone to hell for me at the time, and I lived with them before I had to leave for college. I debated about going early, but Ruth told me how ridiculous that idea was. And after David passed away from a sudden heart attack, we needed each other that summer. When I left for college in Columbia, she came every second weekend, and I would spend all my holidays with her. After that first year, we had both rebuilt our lives, me at university and her here, so we didn't need each other as much anymore. But the bond we created was a lasting one.

"I would go home once a month to her place. When I got back here, I didn't move in with her. I wanted to, but she had grown used to being on her own, and she didn't want some young man to 'cramp her style and be underfoot,' as she told me. I stayed in my own place in town during the week and came here only on the weekends.

"After she died, well, it was hard for me. I still have my parents and extended family, but it's difficult. My mother wants to reform me and bring me back on the right path. As for the rest, we avoid each other. When we can't, things rarely go well. Miss Ruth was like a grandma to me, and I miss her. Being back here, it reminds me of some wonderful things. And brings back the grief, I guess. Though I am happy you didn't change much here, I am puzzled as to why?"

He stopped talking then. From the moment he'd started, I hadn't wanted to interrupt. It looked like he'd needed to get something, whatever it was, off his chest. And to be honest, his warm, sometimes raspy, other times honey-coated voice soothed me, and combined with the hot chocolate and the Bailey's, I felt mellow. I figured out he expected an answer to what I'd thought was a rhetorical question when his gaze didn't leave mine.

"Hm, I am not sure. I think it was a combination of it being a wonderful home, full of heart, which I didn't want to destroy, as well as a deep instinct telling me that the time wasn't right to make big changes here. I try to follow those feelings. The few times I didn't, things went sideways, and sometimes in remarkably preventable ways. Like wearing white pants on an overcast day." He smiled.

"I didn't know about you and Ruth. When I arrived here, I heard people talk, saying it wasn't fair I had inherited the house. I always thought at the time they were talking about the rest of my family. Nobody ever said anything about you and her being close. I am sorry. If I would have known, I would have sold the house to you."

"Don't," he interrupted quietly. "I didn't tell you this story for you to feel bad."

"I promise you I am not feeling sorry for you. I am happy you had someone in your corner. From the gossip I heard and what you just hinted at, I can tell you didn't have much. And we all should. Still, it's not fair to you. She didn't know me, she never met me or my mam, and from what I know, she wasn't ever very fond of her nephews, my dad included. Him, maybe a little less, as he left home young and stayed in Ireland for over twenty years."

I had finished both my drink and the banana bread while he was talking. To occupy my hands, I pulled my knitting basket from under the couch and picked up my latest project at where I had left off. At the quirk of his brow and his smile, I said, "Huh? I learned to knit with my mam when she was sick a long time ago. I kept it up as I hate just sitting in front of the TV, and it beats playing on my phone."

He took another big swallow of his cocoa and a few bites of the bread before talking again.

"Makes sense to me. I watch TV only while eating. Otherwise, I fidget too. Unless I am watching Friends. Then I am good no matter what." He took a big breath before continuing.

"I know you are not aware of it, but Ruth did know you. Or at least she learned about you through your mom. From what Miss Ruthie told me, your mom first started writing to her right after she found out she was pregnant.

"They wrote to each other, usually once a month, unless something big had happened that couldn't wait. Then they would write a second letter or more the same month. In her later years, Miss Ruthie's sight wasn't so good, so she asked me, with your mom's permission, to read and reply to the letters. After they moved to Charleston, your mother made sure to come here a few times.

"A long time ago, I knew Ruth wrote her will with you in mind as her sole heir, and it made sense. One day she called me in and told me she planned to change it. She wanted to share the house between you and me or leave it all to me and some money, but I said no. It wasn't right. What would we do, both of us owning half this house? And me owning it in full felt even worse. She loved me like a grandson, but this property was in David's family for generations, and it should stay in the family."

He grew silent again. I was floored. I had known none of this.

"Jack." I stopped, unsure. "I don't know what to say. Well, yes, I do know. You are always welcome here. No matter what, this door is always open. Literally, when I think about it. I never changed the locks, as her lawyer told me the keys were very old-fashioned and the only ones in existence were the two he was giving me and a third one with the police. At the time, I thought he meant with the office for emergencies. I didn't realize he meant one of the officers.

"I don't know yet how I feel about my mother keeping such

a tremendous thing from me. She is very lucky I don't have my phone. And knowing her, she told Aoibhinn, my sister. As soon as I can get my hands on a SIM card, they better have answers for me.

"Thank you, for telling me and for saying no when she wanted to change her will. I know it's selfish of me, but if you had said yes, then I wouldn't have the home and life I have now. I love it here—this house, the animals, the library, the people I have met and I am now friends with. You. It's just everything I never knew I needed or wanted."

I paused. "There has been something bothering me since we were in the shop earlier. What did the chief and Tom mean about your parents?"

He cleared his throat. "I was outed by one of Jessica's friends when I was eighteen, right after graduation. My parents are very conservative and part of the Baptist church in town, and their views on gay and other LGBTQ people are far from friendly and charitable. My mother has been trying to push me back into 'the right path' ever since. Me not dating isn't helping, I guess."

I snorted, but he looked serious. "What do you mean you don't date? Never? Don't tell me you have been celibate for the past however long since you came back to Weatherboro."

He chuckled at the no doubt horrified look on my face.

"I didn't say I was celibate. I just said I didn't date. It's not like there are a lot of prospects in town. Every now and again, I go out of town to visit old friends in Charleston or Columbia, and I hook up there. What about you? I haven't heard any gossip about you dating either."

I smiled, not sure how much to say. I decided to tell him all. If I wanted to go anywhere with this man, the least I could do was be honest. Whether we would end up friends or more didn't matter.

"I dated when I first arrived. I tried Sam, George, and Marcus. Not all three at the same time, and as you can see, I am not with any of them. Turned out we all want very different things, and none of these things are each other. But I enjoy my friendships with them." I took another sip of my Bailey's. "I downloaded an app a couple of months later, hoping it would help. I met a guy there, and it was going well. I think he was older and, from the way he spoke, probably not out. We were supposed to meet, but he stood me up. When I gave him the address of the restaurant in Weatherboro and he didn't reply, I didn't make much of it. He never showed. When I tried talking to him again, he shut me down pretty fast. I think he probably lives in town, and the fear of being outed was too much for him."

We looked at each other, caught in another stare-off. The cat moving on my lap distracted me, and I put my knitting on the table and looked back at Jack.

His next question didn't surprise me, but the deepness of his voice did. "And now? Are you looking for someone?"

I swallowed. We had moved closer somehow. Almost fully facing Jack, I rested my head on the back of the couch.

"I don't date. That experience was not great, and I am not the biggest fan of apps. I am interested in someone, actually, but I don't think he is ready or wants anything to do with me." I stopped there before the Bailey's and the fatigue deep in my bones made my tongue any looser.

He hummed. I closed my eyes, thinking over what to ask next. I had so many questions.

I must have fallen asleep without noticing and woke up a couple of minutes later when one of the cats jumped down on the floor. My cheek rested on his shoulder. When I looked up and moved back so I could see him, his lovely eyes had grown dark. I could feel the hunger there, and my insides ignited in response.

He bent his head. Where I thought I would get a fiery kiss, like the promise I could see in his gaze, he oh-so-gently brushed his warm lips against mine, tenderly, a few times. It felt so sweet but not enough. The heat was ready to swallow me whole, and grabbing him by the neck, I pulled him closer to me and brushed my tongue against his lips. He let me in, and I took control of the kiss. Pushing my legs under me, I raised onto my knees and took what I needed from him. I caressed his tongue with mine in sweet touches tasting of Bailey's and chocolate. I ran my hands through his hair, pulling gently. The soft whimper that escaped him shot straight to my cock. I needed to hear that sound over and over again.

As I slowly traced down the right side of his body with my left hand, about to raise his shirt, he moved back. We were both panting heavily, and I debated launching myself at him when his phone rang. We jumped away as if burned.

Both trying to catch our breath, we stared at each other while the ringtone of his phone played. Without looking at it, he picked up. The pure horror on his face almost made me laugh. I realized it must have been none other than his mother. After what he had said earlier and our encounter with Jessica, neither the look nor the call surprised me.

I picked up the tray of dirty dishes and walked back to the kitchen. I thought about leaving it for the next day, then decided against it. I wasn't sure how long his call would be, and I didn't want to bear witness to it. I was afraid of the awkwardness waiting for me outside of these walls.

I bent forward, resting my head for a few seconds on the counter in front of the sink. What had I done? I mean, it was everything I had been dreaming of for a while, and I had a nagging sense of déjà vu. And thinking back, he'd initiated it. But this would complicate things. We both needed some time to process it. I cleaned the dishes, trying to not think about anything at all. Instead, I focused on what plants I needed to add to the front of the house and which vegetables and fruits I needed to sow this weekend that I hadn't already.

Done, I prepared myself to go to the sitting room when I heard a soft noise at the kitchen entryway. I turned around to find Jack there staring at me.

## 10

JACK

**Still Friday - Night**

As brief as it had been, that was one uncomfortable conversation with my mother. She hadn't said hello; she'd started yelling at me right away. How unseemly it was they had caught me with that man at the supermarket. How I dared make her look like a fool in front of Jessica by pretending I didn't know what she was talking about and trying to get out of my duties.

For once, I let her talk. I would normally cut her off pretty quickly if I picked up at all. Today I didn't mind. I was so lost in that kiss. It had been everything. His falling asleep and leaning on my shoulder. An old song playing on the radio. When I'd turned it on, the station had surprised me, and I knew it wasn't that Ruth or I had left it on that particular one two years ago. I was looking forward to discovering more things about him I didn't know.

When the cat jumped off his lap and he startled awake, the softness in his eyes, the vulnerability there, had done me in.

Thibault had a strength in him I couldn't wait to explore if he'd allow me to. The kiss had started out soft, melting me into him. When he took control, passion had exploded through me. His dominant side was rearing its head. I'd had the pleasure of seeing it in action almost a year ago, and I'd happily relinquished the reins. His hands in my hair drew noises out of me that would have made me cringe if I was with anyone else, but not with Thibault. I knew he would not judge. Quite the contrary, it spurred him on.

The guilt came rearing back. What we had done was everything I wanted—hell, I'd started it. But he was still a suspect in our investigation, and the things he didn't know, combined with everything else, might make him pull away from me. The shrill voice of my mother calling my name brought me back to the present.

"Yes, Mother?" I replied, somewhat more mildly than she deserved. She had stopped something great from progressing further. I'd pulled back, more to regain a little control and much-needed breath than to stop what had been a fiery kiss. I wouldn't have been strong enough to stop if he'd come in for seconds. With everything going on, I was glad for the interruption. Even though I would have definitely preferred anyone else on the phone than her.

"Did you listen to a word I said? This is unacceptable. I have had enough of this nonsense, Jack. You will call Jessica this week and meet with her. It's about time you two settled down. And I expect to see her on your arm at the mayor's celebration next month, are we clear?"

I debated how to answer. Oh, I was going. Who came with me was another question. It for sure wouldn't be Jessica. "Oh, don't worry, Mother, I will be at the mayor's ball. There is no doubt about that. You just interrupted one of the best moments of my life with a wonderful man, so if you will excuse me, I'll get right back to him. Have a wonderful night, Mother. Goodbye."

I hung up and put her number on the Do Not Disturb list as I knew she would call right back. Because the station might need me, I couldn't turn my phone off or put it on silent. And I didn't want my phone ringing off the hook for the next hour. Or until my father had had enough of my mother's pacing and screaming at my answering machine and took her phone away.

Water was running in the kitchen, so I went that way to check on him. It was barely ten o'clock. I felt weary—the day, the kiss, the conversation all weighing on me.

I stopped at the entrance to the kitchen and looked at Thibault. His back was to me. I was about to clear my throat or make a noise to alert him to my presence when he turned around. At first, he seemed a little surprised. Then his face cleared, and he smiled. I couldn't help the answering smile on my face before I schooled my features. I needed to take a step back, and if I smiled or moved toward him, things would pick up right where we'd left off. I wasn't ready yet.

"I am going to turn in now. Thank you for the food and the company. If you need anything, just shout. I am a light sleeper. You should feel better in the morning, and I can recommend a psychologist who can help you work through what you saw. I will give you his number when you come in for your statement. Goodnight."

Before he could retort, I turned around and went down the corridor faster than necessary. I picked up my bag, left at the bottom of the stairs earlier, and went into the bathroom, brushed my teeth, and washed my face. I then entered the room I used to sleep in. I didn't switch on the light, just chucked my clothes near the left side of the bed and dove in, placing my phone on the bedside table. This day needed to end.

I tried falling asleep but couldn't. My mind kept replaying the kiss, Jessica, Thibault, my mother, Ruth, the murder. It was all starting to spiral in a blur. I was on my fifth toss and turn, plumping my pillow, when the lamp on the opposite side of the bed switched on. Thibault was wearing only a pair of loose sleep pants. The soft light and shadows played on his chest and muscled arms. He looked mouthwatering. I might have growled.

He rolled his eyes, smirked at me, and went under the covers. The bed dipped at the end as Spot and Scout joined us. Scout curled into a ball between our feet, and Spot came to rest between the two pillows.

"What are you doing, Thibault? Did you need something?"

"Relax, Detective, I don't need anything, and I got the message loud and clear in the kitchen. It was a mistake, it shouldn't happen again, you're sorry you took advantage of my vulnerable moment, blah blah blah. Trust me when I say I don't care, and I am not here for that. I am guessing this was the guest room you used to sleep in, correct?"

I nodded, unsure what else to do or say.

"Well, even though I haven't changed much in the house, at least downstairs, I made changes upstairs. I didn't feel comfortable using the room Ruth used as her bedroom. And as this room is the biggest, I am using it as my bedroom. Now stop making that face. I don't care where you sleep. If you wish, you can stay right here, or not. I won't jump your bones and steal your virtue. Have no fear, Detective. You are safe with me. Now stop jumping around. I'd like to sleep. Goodnight." He turned around, switched off the light, and fell asleep.

I lay still, debating what to do. His soft breathing mixed

with the animals, the warmth of the duvet, the pitter-patter of the rain on the window, and the wind in the trees lulled me to sleep.

I startled awake to Lady Gaga and a warm body moving against me. A hand stroked my hair gently. "Shhh, you're all right, Jack. Go back to sleep." I drifted back to unconscious bliss. What felt like a second later, my phone went off. Rihanna, here to remind me it was time to stand up. I sat on the bed for a few seconds trying to recenter myself.

I looked around. This room definitely wasn't mine. The bed was king-sized with pretty white flowery sheets and smelled of lavender and pine. I knew that smell. Thibault. The walls were a deep blue with light green accents. And the furniture was a light brown I remembered well. The pictures on the bedside table featured Thibault with his family and friends. I heard sounds downstairs, which was where my host must have been. I stood up, heading in the bathroom's direction, when I noticed the closet door was open.

The detective in me reared his head, and I needed to look. Not that anyone with half a mind would leave bloody clothes there, but you never knew. Especially if, in their panic, they tossed the evidence in the closet and didn't expect a detective to invite himself to sleep in their bed. Hell, I felt like a moron. Thibault was right. I should have asked last night instead of going off like a coward and hiding in his bedroom.

I peeked inside. There were slacks, jeans, and shirts but no blood-covered shoes or clothes. A box to my left held what looked like letters. Intrigued and nosier than usual, I glanced at one. Before I read more than the first sentence—*Dear Thibault, You looked beautiful today.*—I noticed something else in his closet and dropped the letter back.

It had nothing to do with murder. It made my blood roar down fast, waking up my settling morning wood. A harness. A stunning black shoulder harness. Different to the one he wore at Pride. Hope bloomed through me. I was lost in thoughts. Did this mean the first one hadn't been just an accessory or gag gift, and what might it mean?

A sound came from behind me. Turning around, I found Thibault at the door, gazing at me with an amused look on his face. "Found something you like, Detective?" I blushed and shrugged. "I heard your alarm and thought I would pop up and see if you were awake. I changed some things in the bathroom, but I am sure you can figure it out. There are fresh towels. Come down when you are ready, and I'll jump in. I forgot to switch off my alarm, so I am making breakfast."

He turned around and went back downstairs. Grabbing my bag, I went into the bathroom. I hadn't noticed last night, but it had changed. It was retiled, and the color scheme was now blue with fishes and shellfish for both the walls and the shower stall. The stall itself appeared much bigger. I was happy to note he'd kept the antique copper bathtub, which was now opposite the shower.

After chucking down my boxers and shirt, I went into the shower. It had two different heads, a traditional one and one of these rain versions. After some fumbling with the different dials and getting sprayed in the face by some icy water, I was able to make it work and enjoyed a very warm and relaxing shower. I bypassed my erection; touching it didn't feel right. And I had the feeling I was running late—no need adding to it.

I exited the shower and took a towel from the warmer, another new addition. It wasn't cold in the room, but being wrapped in a fluffy warm towel was wonderful. I might try convincing my landlord to go fifty-fifty on one for my own bathroom. I brushed my teeth and combed my beard and hair after running some of my products through them. I wasn't vain, or at least I tried not to be, but I loved taking care of myself. Another one of those things my parents drilled into me from a young age: always look presentable. This one I enjoyed doing.

I looked into my bag to grab a clean shirt, uniform, and underwear. Blushing, I noticed which ones I had picked up. I would have to pray that, today of all days, nothing would make me undress in public. Yesterday my brain had decided we would get lucky or something. One of my sexiest pairs of underwear was dangling from my fingers, a black lace jock-strap. I had purchased it online at my favorite store. It could have been worse. At least this one was comfortable and supportive. While I love wearing these on my days off, I never ever did on workdays. You never knew what could happen.

I put it on. The other option was going commando, and there was no way I would do that at work. Feeling naughty, I then put on the rest of my clothes.

I folded and stuffed my dirty clothes back into my bag and went back to the bedroom. I picked up the things left on the floor and my cell phone and went downstairs. Dropping my bag near the front door, I made my way to the kitchen. It smelled heavenly and like nothing I would usually eat for breakfast. A longer workout tonight and tomorrow was in the cards.

I stopped at the entrance, taking in the view in front of me. The back door was open, the cats and dogs coming and going as they pleased. Thibault was at the stove, singing his head off, shaking his hips in time with the rhythm of a hard rock song. This definitely wasn't something I listened to, being more of a pop or country guy myself. But I wasn't surprised after seeing rock band T-shirts in his wardrobe this morning and the soft rock station yesterday.

Using the spoon he was stirring with as a microphone, he

turned around, dancing, wearing only his sleep pants. Bare-foot and bare-chested seemed to be his favorite thing. I would not complain; it was definitely a marvelous view. Seeing me, he shut up mid-word.

"Oh, please, don't stop on my account. At least you can carry a tune better than I do. And the dancing was delightful." His eyes widened. I wasn't sure if it was at my sudden playfulness or being caught. But reactions so far to my newfound cheerfulness denoted a lot of surprise.

"If you think these were impressive moves, Detective, you are in for a surprise the day you get the privilege to see me truly dance." I knew already how he looked when he danced with intent, and he was glorious. Not that he was aware. "Please sit down instead of towering in the doorway. Coffee black with a dash of milk, right?"

I smiled. We had a tendency to run (literally or not) into each other at the coffee shop, as we both enjoyed the goods of the Miracle Brew. And even though my preference wasn't special or complicated, it warmed me to know he had noticed. I nodded as I took a seat. "I can..."

"Don't worry." He cut me off as he poured me a cup of fresh coffee, then added a drop of milk.

He walked back to the stove and switched it off. A few seconds later, I had a bowl full of porridge in front of me. On the table was toast, two hard-boiled eggs, bacon and ham, jam, honey, and other things.

"Please help yourself to anything. I heard you say you usually take porridge. Hope I made it right. I am more of an egg-and-bacon guy myself. But my mam keeps on telling me I need to take care of my cholesterol, so these are turkey rashers. Next to the jams is some compote I removed from the freezer. It's all homemade. Blackberry and red currant for the jam, apricot, peaches, and persimmon for the compote with a dash of cinnamon. Salt and pepper are here if you are more of a salty porridge kind of guy."

He was so thoughtful. I grabbed the compote and put some on toast. Biting into it, I moaned at the taste. This was delicious. I had never tasted persimmon this way before. I scooped a big dollop and put it in my porridge, adding jam on the rest of my toast. I ate without pausing. After a few mouthfuls, I took in my surroundings. Thibault was going through his bacon and egg, watching me with an amused smile on his lips. "Sorry. I do cook but nothing like this. It tastes so good. I couldn't resist."

"That's all right. I like nothing more than a man with an appetite." He went back to his own breakfast, and we both finished at a more sedate pace.

Once done, we brought our dishes to the sink. Thibault moved to wash them, and I nudged him away. "Why don't you go shower while I do this? If you are ready when I am done, we can go to town together so you can get your car. Is that all right?"

"If you are sure?" At my nod, he left me to it, shouting on his way out, "I'll be quick, promise."

I took the rest of the utensils and cookware he had used to make us breakfast and washed and dried it all before placing everything back where it belonged.

Once finished, I went to the entrance to put on my shoes. That was when I saw his shoe rack. Debating with myself, I looked up toward the bathroom. The part of me falling for Thibault told me to not do it. The detective's voice, just as it had when seeing his wardrobe, was stronger. As the shower was still going, I pulled my phone out. Taking his shoes one by one, I snapped pictures of the soles. I was so absorbed in the task I didn't hear the water switch off, or the door open, or Thibault coming down the stairs.

He shouted, "What the fuck are you doing with my shoes?" He was ready to go and had caught me red-handed. Even if one of these shoes matched the prints we had lifted at either crime scene, it was inadmissible evidence. Marcus was right. I was so twisted over this—I was screwed.

I lifted back up. Fury was written all over Thibault's face. "Detective, I will only ask you once. What the hell are you doing looking through my shoes?" I had two choices. Either tell a bold-faced lie neither of us would believe or give him the truth and face the consequences.

"I was taking pictures of your shoes. We found shoe prints at both our crimes scenes."

"So you thought while I was otherwise occupied, you would take it upon yourself to check without asking? And then what? Check against your prints at the station, then come back with a warrant once you found the proof I was guilty?

"Was that what you were looking for in my closet earlier? Bloody clothes, bloody shoes? Was this your plan all along, just come in under the guise of helping someone out, be all nice and sweet, and then snoop around until you find proof I killed Sally Anne?"

I was feeling so stupid no retort came to mind. His look, a mix of disappointed, horrified, and a little sad, broke my heart. If my running away from him last night after our kiss wasn't enough, my actions this morning definitely put a stop to whatever had started between us. And even though I should have felt relieved, I was ashamed and depressed.

In a soft voice, he continued. "I see. Why don't you take your pictures and your things and get out of my house? I will find my way into town. And don't bother coming back. If you get a warrant to search through some more of my things, you can send one of your deputies to do that for you." He turned on his heels and ran back upstairs.

I stared after him. Yes, I was an idiot. I grabbed my bag, pocketed my phone, and pulled out my keys. I took a few steps on the stairs and stopped. I didn't know what to say. How to make him understand why. It had nothing to do with us, though after this, I would be lucky if there was even friendship on offer. I turned around and left.

**11**

---

THIBAULT

**Saturday, April 13, 2019**

he water falling over me felt nice, relaxing even. This morning was so wonderfully domestic. Waking up held by powerful arms and plastered along Jack's strong body was something I hadn't know I craved. Deep down, it was the man as much as the feeling of waking up with someone. I soaked in his heat and would have fallen back asleep if it hadn't been for my alarm.

We had a silent but enjoyable breakfast. Seeing him enjoy what I made felt good. I was lucky to have such an impressive garden. Once finished, I agreed to his offer of cleaning for me while I showered.

I made my way downstairs, stopping on the last step. Jack was taking pictures of the soles of my shoes, shattering my sunny morning. I stayed still for a few seconds, thinking I was mistaken. I wasn't. At least his answers were honest. Anger and heartbreak coursed through me. Before I could calm down, I threw him out.

I was now pacing in my room, waiting for him to leave. I was so proud of myself. I hadn't screamed or slammed doors. Go me! I had preserved my dignity. But now I felt worse than yesterday. I was shaking with anger, tears welling up in my eyes from the hurt. I choked it back. Footsteps on the stairs receded quickly, soon followed by the sound of the door closing. I felt it slam against my heart, closing the door on what I'd felt last night.

I heard the sound of a motor outside. Looking out the window, I watched his car leave. Hearing him on the stairs had felt the worst somehow. It had given me hope, even if for a second, that he regretted it. That hope vanished as his truck disappeared down the road.

I slumped against the windowsill, taking a deep breath to calm down. I was torn between running after him to shake some sense into him and washing my hands of this whole thing. I wiped at the tear that fell, despite my trying to not let any escape. He wasn't worth crying over. I tried to reason with my heart. All we had was one kiss and two years of back and forth, not even close to flirting. There was nothing to cry over. But the anger I couldn't get rid of so easily. Who did he think he was, coming here and trying to find proof of my murdering someone?

Feeling a cat rub and purr against my legs, I looked down to see Sandy. My girl wasn't always the friendliest of all the cats. But I learned long ago she was very intuitive and knew when I needed a friendly reminder that things were okay. And I had her and her friends to feed. Not that I hadn't feed them earlier, but cats were always so hungry. Bottomless pits, the lot of them.

Squaring my shoulders, I changed into what I considered my work clothes—an old pair of jeans, an even older T-shirt, and my boots—and went outside to the paddocks. It was a little later than I usually tried to arrive, and the complaints were audible from here. I fed everyone, then cleaned their stalls. New hay, clean water, extra feed. It took me a few hours, but it felt good. At first, I tried to ignore everything that had happened in the past twenty-four hours, but it wasn't working. So I went through it bit by bit, starting with what I'd found yesterday morning. There was definitely nothing I could have done for Sally Anne.

I could understand why someone would think I was responsible, but it hurt that Jack would be one of the first ones to point it out. When I thought about it rationally, it made sense. I could have lured her to the duck pond or simply happened upon her there and gotten into another argument. Things could have escalated and boom. To take suspicion away from me, I would have moved her to the library. My prints were there. I had a key, but so did Sally Anne. It seemed far-fetched and too easy. He could have asked, couldn't he? Not outright, I guessed. If I had murdered her, I would deny it. But it would have been nicer than snooping.

Now, who actually had done it was another question. I wasn't an amateur sleuth or private detective and wouldn't even try. I enjoyed crime fiction, and true crime fascinated me. I watched every crime show I could put my hands on. I'd gone as far as minoring in criminology in college. I knew how much detectives, or law enforcement in general, hated it when the public thought they could solve things on their own. Eight times out of ten it ended in heartache, disaster, or both.

But this had my curiosity piqued as well as my pride some-how, and it wouldn't hurt to think about it. From what I knew, Sally Anne was well liked by her cronies at the church and the HPS but not appreciated by anyone else. She was single and didn't have any direct family still living around here. So, that left a lot of suspects. Ah, well. I hoped they found out who did it, and people wouldn't discover I was a potential suspect. Or that it wouldn't have any adverse effect on my reputation or the library's.

My mind, free to jump to something else, latched on to the kiss. That had been, well, wonderful. It had started sweet, growing gradually hotter. I had enjoyed it so much, and if it hadn't been for that phone call interrupting us, I know I would have pushed for more. Yesterday it had disappointed me. Right now, I was delighted things hadn't gone further. I could move on from a kiss, maybe. I mean, I still hadn't moved on from the one I'd shared with my mystery man a year ago.

That one had started softly as well. Both times initiated by a man much taller and stronger than me. Both came in fast and became soft and sweet.

Wait. Bells had rung in my head last night, but half-dazed from the sensations, I hadn't paid them any attention. It was the exact same kiss—the lips, warmth, softness—just a different angle. And like that, all my anger, rage, and sadness I'd pushed back down using rationalization came back tenfold.

How dared he? Not only did he think I'd murdered some-one, but for the past year he'd hidden being the man I was looking for since Pride. I remembered clear as day when he caught me sighing about the "mystery" man for the millionth time to Sam and George. Exasperated, Sam had told me to either stop dating altogether or fuck anything that moved to get him out of my system. George had added, though more nicely than Sam would have, that the chances of me finding him in Weatherboro were close to nil as I was in Charleston when we met. If you could call a passionate encounter a meeting.

I didn't know what to think anymore. Was it so bad he chose not to see where it could go? Was yesterday a moment of weakness? Just satiating a need with a willing body, feeling no spark on his side? Or was he so scared he kept running, and this investigation was another way of putting more barriers between us when the old ones crumbled?

After I finished the last enclosure, I stomped back inside and removed all my clothes in the kitchen. That had become a habit of mine pretty quickly, and unless Steve was here, I usually dropped trou right where I stood, on the steps or just inside the door. My washing machine and dryer were next to the kitchen, and I didn't see the point tracking mud or dirt throughout the house.

Once naked, I put everything in the laundry basket I left downstairs, retrieved my clothes from yesterday from the dryer, and brought them upstairs with me. After dumping them on the bed, I went into the shower. If I had known what the morning would entail, I wouldn't have bothered and wasted water.

Once I was done showering again, I went back down and picked up the house phone. Ruth had had a few installed in different rooms. One in the sitting room, one in the kitchen, and one in the bedroom upstairs. When I'd first moved in, I'd programmed numbers in them. Now I selected the one I needed.

The call connected. "Weatherboro Police Department, George speaking. How may I help you?"

"Hey, George, it's Thibault."

"Thibault, are you all right?"

I chuckled. "I am fine, George. This call is nothing like yesterday's. Though if a certain someone had stayed a little longer this morning, there might have been another dead body to collect, and this time everyone would know who'd done it. I am supposed to come in to give my prints, but I am home without my car as I got a lift yesterday. What time should I come in?"

"Oh, good. You had me worried there for a second. I can put you in for the early afternoon and check if Jack is around, if you'd like?"

"As weird as it might sound, I would prefer not to give my deposition or prints to Detective Tomlins. I already recounted my story to him yesterday. I don't want to bother him."

"You're so sweet and thoughtful. Jack is grumpier than a cat going through catnip withdrawal today. So different from last night. I will make sure Marcus is available to take care of you when you come in this afternoon."

"Perfect, thank you very much. I'll see you later."

Once I hung up, I called Sam's phone. He usually had his afternoon free on Saturdays and was off on Sundays unless it was market day.

"Hey, Thibault, what's up, sweetie?"

"Hey, Sam, would you mind coming over by my house? I need a lift to town to retrieve my car and head to the police station to go over my statement and give them my prints."

"Sure thing, sweetie. That's no problem. I should be finished in the next few minutes. I'll come around in about one hour if that's all right. If you didn't stop by the shop when picking up your car, I planned on coming to see you today. I need details, sweet cheeks."

I laughed. Did it sound bitter? Yeah, most likely, but at this stage, I didn't care. "An hour is grand. It gives me just the right time to get ready for you. I'll see you then."

I made my way upstairs to the smallest room of the house, which I'd transformed into an office of sorts. This was the one room I had changed so far in the house. When I moved in, it had contained only a small bed and old broken things. I put most of that in the shed to repair or bring to the landfill, and I had completed a few minor projects with the wood I'd reclaimed. The room was small, but I put in a cabinet, a corner desk, and a chest of drawers. The room itself was a light blue with lines of dark green interspersed. The furniture was black and sturdy.

I had the feeling my old mobile was stashed somewhere in this room. I tended to relegate anything electronic here. I first checked the chest of drawers on the left. Rummaging through the drawers, I was able to find the phone. The screen was cracked, but it would do for the few days or weeks the police department had my mobile. I opened it quickly, not remembering if I'd asked for a new SIM or not when I'd upgraded. I was happy to see one inside. With a bit of luck, my contacts would be saved here and the only thing to do would be to transfer my number back.

I put it to charge on the multi-plug on my desk. I started my computer and checked out the number for the local store. After a quick call with them, I was informed that no, it wouldn't be a problem to transfer my number and to restart the phone after a few hours. If nothing changed, I needed to call back on Monday.

As my PC was on, I checked my emails and searched what to do when you were a suspect in a murder investigation. I knew what was on the Internet should be taken with a grain of salt, but I needed to start somewhere. It said to be as cooperative as possible, and that if things started heating up, I should get an attorney to navigate the situation.

I looked up the number for Aunt Ruth's attorney to see if he could help or recommend someone. When I called, his secretary told me he should be able to take my call straightaway and transferred me. "This is Kenneth Miller. How may I help you?"

"Hi, Mr. Miller, this is Thibault Abrams. You handled the

will of Ruth Turner, my great-aunt. Could you spare a few minutes to answer some questions?"

"Of course. Do you want to make your will or do something specific with your current assets?"

"Nothing like that. I am embroiled in a murder investigation. It looks like I am either being set up or simple circumstances are pointing in my direction as the main suspect of a crime I didn't commit. I don't know if I need legal representation already or what I need to do."

"All right, I see. Let me start by saying this is not my area of expertise. I handled such cases in my youth, as at the time, it was a little less specialized, especially in small towns. We now have two other attorneys on board in our practice, and I leave these cases to them. But you must remember to omit nothing, no matter how it might look. And cooperate. I can refer you to my colleague, so if you are going in for an interview with the police or they take you into custody, you have someone there to guide you."

"Thank you. If you could give me their name and phone number, I will see how things go at the station today. Another question I have is this. If I knew the police found certain things at the crime scene, should I provide them with evidence it wasn't me?"

"I wouldn't if I were you. They might take it two ways. Either you are guilty and playing with them, or you are innocent and think the police cannot do their jobs. In either case, it won't help you. As for the statement, make sure you give it a thorough read-through before signing anything."

"Thank you, Mr. Miller. I appreciate this."

"No problem at all, young man. Here is the phone number of my colleague. His name is Harold Standrom, and I will let him know you might call him." I grabbed a pen and paper and wrote the details. Thanking him profusely for his help and counsel, I hung up.

I stared into space for a few moments. I won't lie—I'd considered storming in and dropping all of my shoes on Jack's desk while giving him a piece of my mind. Now that I had talked to Mr. Miller, my anger receded a little. Yes, I was mightily pissed off at Jack; it felt like that arse was playing me, and he definitely was lying to me far too easily. But I had to concentrate. I was a suspect in a very serious murder investigation. Not that murder was ever not serious.

So I would need to remain calm and act like the professional adult person I was. I snorted. Just that the sentence sounded so adult, not. It didn't matter. I would do my best, and if things went wrong or got worse, then I would call Mr. Standrom. All I knew was Jack had been checking the soles of my shoes. Either he was trying to prove I was innocent or trying to convince himself I was guilty. When I went to the precinct, I would see what reaction I received.

I switched off the computer and took my mobile and charger downstairs, feeling hungry.

On my way to the kitchen, I noticed the letter I left on the commode last night. I picked it up. I knew exactly who it was from, but I didn't want to open it. Well, I didn't know who they were, but I was familiar enough with the paper and envelope to know they came from my "secret admirer."

Hoping on Thursday these had stopped had been wishful thinking on my part. They had started sweet at first but became increasingly creepier in the past few months. I'd had the feeling of being watched every now and again. I'd never gone to the police with the letters. I knew I should have approached Marcus or Jack with them. But I knew there was no point.

I'd always thought they might be coming from the man I'd

met through the app. He'd ghosted me a couple weeks before they started coming in. One of the cases we studied during my criminology course was that sometimes going to the police might trigger the stalker by either angering them or making them feel betrayed. Usually, things ended badly for the victim. I didn't want to become another statistic.

Receiving it on a Friday night instead of the usual Thursday shouldn't have meant anything, but I had the feeling things were about to change for me and not just because of Sally Anne's murder.

I shook myself off and dropped it back into the glass bowl where I usually kept my keys.

Trying to quell the shudder racing down my spine, I made my way to the kitchen. Dread had cut down my appetite, but I ate anyway. I couldn't let it affect me; it wouldn't help.

## 12

THIBAULT

**Saturday - Midday**

When Sam arrived, I was raring to go. I needed this day to be over. I kept telling myself that it would be all right and everything I had discovered so far was fine. I would definitely need to do yoga and clean my garden later. Knitting wouldn't cut it—it wouldn't take my mind off things—but gardening was very therapeutic for me and, combined with yoga, often helped clear my head.

I didn't let Sam get out of his car, instead going straight in. "Hey. Thank you so much for doing this."

"You know that's no problem, right? It's not like you haven't helped me countless times before and always refused help in return. I am happy to do this for you. And like I said earlier, I want details."

I smiled. I knew he wouldn't repeat what I told him to anyone, especially intimate details, but right now I wasn't sure I wanted to share.

"Ok, hmm, things didn't go the way you assume. And right

now I really don't know how I feel about any of it or everything that happened in the past twenty-four hours." He looked concerned but nodded and started slowly driving back to the main road.

"All right, sweetie, I understand. How about going for drinks tonight?"

I nodded. "Sounds good to me. I'll ask George if he is free, so I can tell you both at the same time."

"Perfect, sweetie. Now, just a warning, people noticed you were shopping with Jack last night. That piece of gossip made the rounds, especially how he turned down Jessica. Tabitha stopped by the shop this morning to escape Jessica's foul mood. Jack's equally grim mood is making the rumors go wild.

"And I know who was murdered yesterday. Sally Anne. I can't believe it. Dorothy is apparently heartbroken and is telling people you did it. She is not too vocal about it, so either she must know it's not you or she knows something else is at play here. What if she did it and is using you as a scapegoat? Anyway, consensus around town is you didn't do it. It would be stupid for you to kill Sally Anne and then drop her at your place of work."

I replied with a chuckle. "Thank you. That helps. Jack told me about Sally Anne last night. The Dorothy part is ludicrous, and you know it. I am trying not to speculate on people's opinions right now. I can't shake the idea of a mob of people with pitchforks running me out of town." This time we both laughed.

We arrived in town and parked at the library. "Thanks for the ride, love. That was very sweet of you. Now the police station, and then I am going straight home. You take care, and I'll talk to you tonight at the Tavern. I won't stay long as we have market tomorrow, but a drink sounds phenomenal."

"Good luck, sweetie. And call me anytime for anything—you know I am always here."

"I know, and you can't understand how much I appreciate you." I left the car and waved goodbye.

Going into the station, I took a deep breath and almost ran into John. He chuckled and made way. Yeah, I didn't only plow into Jack. Other people got the chance to bump into me too. Awkward, me? Never. Equal opportunist to distribute free hugs? Always.

I smiled. "Hey, John."

He passed me, talking over his shoulder. "Hey, Thibault. Hope you're doing okay after yesterday. I gotta run—calls to answer, people to help. You know the drill." And he was gone. He'd never rattled on with me before. What had him so flustered? Near George's desk, I noticed a tall form retreating farther into the police station. Jack. Great.

I walked toward the front desk. Seeing me, George rushed around and engulfed me in a hug.

"Hey, Thibault, how are you doing? I can't even imagine what you are going through. You should have called yesterday evening. I could have stayed with you at your place."

I returned his hug, then taking a step back, answered, "It's okay, love. I am fine. I had company. Actually, would you like to come out tonight to the Tavern? I am going with Sam for some drinking and talking. Unless you are planning another typewriter hunting trip?"

He looked surprised, his brows raised in question. Then he smiled. "Nope, I think I have enough of those. I bought two new ones to replace the one stolen last year. Don't try to confuse me with the typewriter comment. I see, the rumors were true about you and Jack. You need a drink, and he is crankier than usual. I definitely am in for tonight. Now, business. Why don't you go to the conference room? It's down the corridor to your right. I'll have Marcus come over to take your prints and statement."

"Thank you."

I went in the direction he indicated. A sign said Conference Room to the side of an open door, so I went in. The room was medium-sized with a round table seating twelve people, more if you squeezed in, with chairs that were sturdy and not comfortable. The walls were a light gray, which definitely didn't inspire joy. I hoped Marcus wouldn't be too long. This room was depressing.

Was it on purpose? Reflecting on it, they held their meetings here, so probably not. For their sake, I hoped the rest of the precinct had cheerier colors.

Hearing footsteps, I lifted my head as Marcus came in. He was always bigger than life, a huge smile on his face. After we went on our only date, we decided to stay friends. I wasn't close to him like I was with George and Sam, but I enjoyed his company. We tried to grab drinks at least once a month. Being around him was always fun. It was a pity there was no chemistry between us, as he was tall and handsome and full of life.

"Hey, T, how are you doing today? Recovered a little?"

I smiled. "I am doing all right, despite the circumstances. And yourself?"

"I am well, thanks. So let's get started. Is it all right if I record this?"

"Go ahead." Been there, done that, got the T-shirt yesterday. And it wasn't like I had any big revelations to add to my statement.

"I know you already explained what happened, but could you please repeat it for me again, with as much detail as possible?"

"Sure thing."

He put the recorder on the table and started. "This is

Detective Marcus Elmer with witness Thibault Abrams today for his statement. Could you please tell me what happened?"

Once again, I recounted the events of Friday morning, starting from leaving the coffee shop to the moment the police arrived. Then came the fun question time.

"Thibault, could you please tell me what you did the night before? From 7:00 p.m. until you found the body."

"I finished my shift at the library at about 5:00 p.m. as it wasn't my time to close. I went on home. After feeding my zoo, I had dinner, then stayed in my sitting room for an hour watching TV, then went to bed. I woke up at six thirty the next morning and left around seven thirty. I believe I was at Sam's at seven forty-five and got to the library a little before eight."

"Thank you, Thibault. Anyone who can corroborate the times?"

"For the night, no, I was alone. For the morning... well, Steve, the ranch hand from one of the neighboring farms, comes in around six thirty to take care of my animals during the week, so he would have been there and could have seen the car, or if anyone came up to the farm before I left, I guess. After that, I would say Sam, Detective Tomlins, and everyone at the café."

"Do you have any cameras or an alarm system to confirm you were home last night?"

"No, I don't. Unless Detective Tomlins installed one for Ruth before she passed that I don't know about, then no, there is nothing to show I was home, apart from, like I said earlier, Steve in the early hours of the morning. Am I a suspect, Detective? Or under arrest? Should I contact my lawyer?"

He startled a bit at "Detective." "What? No, Thibault, what are you talking about? This is standard procedure. We need as many details as we can to create a timeframe. And the prints are to eliminate you from the ones we lifted in places where your prints would normally be."

"Oh, really? Will you be asking the same questions of Charlene or the others from the library?"

He fidgeted. I had learned a lot through my criminology courses, and if I'd had the guts, I would have gone into criminal justice or become a lawyer. But early on, I realized working in law would either consume me or destroy me. Probably both. His looking a little antsy showed me I had made him uncomfortable. So, even though his demeanor was friendly, he considered me a suspect as well. Did they really have no other leads?

"Thibault, I can't say more than I am allowed—you know that. We need to cover all our bases. You found the body of a woman who you argued with on a regular basis, including the day before the murder. It's not much in the grand scheme of things, but we need to check all avenues. Either to eliminate you completely from the suspect pool or to pursue this further. And to be honest, I don't believe you did it. I am sure what we have so far will prove it, but until we find an actual suspect or rule you out thanks to the evidence, I would say you are a person of interest. I don't think you need a lawyer, but it wouldn't hurt to consult one. Lord, Jack will kill me for explaining this to you."

I nodded, understanding. Nothing I could do about it.

He continued. "Now, let me grab the kit, and I'll take your prints."

I waited for him to come back and let him get what he needed. When he switched off the recording, I asked, "Is Jack in?"

"I assume so. Do you want me to check?"

"No, that's all right. Thanks, Marcus."

He smiled at me. "Sure thing. Listen, things are weird,

confusing, and hard to deal with right now. Give it some time, and it will get better. Please call me if you remember anything, all right? And we will contact you if we need any other information."

"I will. Enjoy your day and take care, Marcus."

On my way toward the exit, I spotted Jack hovering in front of an empty room. I pushed him inside and closed the door behind me without giving him the chance to react.

He seemed surprised to see me. I stared at him for a second. With him here, the wind left my sails, and I didn't know where to start. I had been full of righteous rage earlier, but now I felt empty.

"You shouldn't have done that this morning, Jack. If anything matches, it won't be admissible in court, as you got it without my permission. You should know better than to make such an idiotic mistake. You are letting your need to push me away cloud your judgment. I was hurt and angry when I kicked you out. Now, I don't know what to think or feel anymore.

"I have been attracted to you for quite some time. Between what I heard about you around town and glimpses of the true you, you intrigued me. I thought you hated me for whatever reason. But yesterday, things changed. Last night was something I didn't expect, but I was happy. I discovered a different side of you and understood more of what's happened between us in the past two years.

"After you left this morning, I spent quite some time pondering all this. One thing frustrating me was the feeling I was missing something. A thought at the back of my mind, barely out of reach. And then it clicked. You were my mystery stranger. One of the best moments of my life. I wasn't wearing a mask, and my friend called me by my name before my mystery man disappeared. Afterward, I convinced myself the flash of recognition I had seen in my mystery man's face was just a reflection of the light. But you knew exactly who I was. Everything happening is now much clearer and more muddled than ever.

"I won't say I know or understand your reasons, and to be honest, right now I don't want to hear them. If your team needs something further from me for the investigation, they better ask or come with a warrant or you won't get anything from me. As for the rest..."

He jumped in at that. "Last night was a lapse in judgment. Whether or not you killed Sally Anne, you are a person of interest in this investigation, and nothing can happen between us."

"Thank you for the interruption. As I started saying, even if after all these revelations, a relationship was still on the table, now is not the right time. You wouldn't trust me, and I definitely wouldn't trust you. So for the time being, no contact would be better. You have enough people here to talk to me without us interacting. And then, well, we will see."

I nodded and left without letting him add anything.

There was nothing left for us to say. It wouldn't help; it would only make things harder and more confusing. And I wouldn't put myself, or him, through that. There was no point. One of us needed to be rational, and I wanted him to concentrate on the investigation. Selfish or not, I needed this closed, for Sally Anne's sake and my own.

I left the building, reminding George on my way out to meet me around 6:00 p.m. at the Tavern, and made my way home. Gardening, cooking, cleaning—anything would do to keep my mind off things until I could get a drink. I hoped.

**Jack**

Despite wanting to stop Thibault, I didn't. He was right, and how crazy was that? Me, king of the rules and doing it by the book—I was just reminded by someone I considered a suspect to keep things professional and put my head back in the game.

Today was not pleasant. When I arrived, everyone teased me because the news of my shopping trip with Thibault had gone through town as fast as Wile E. Coyote on a rocket. They all discovered today was not the day to make jokes when they saw my scowl getting deeper by the second.

The new voicemail from my mother on my work phone had soured my mood further. Marcus had returned to the duck pond this morning with John while I stayed back looking for clues on Sally Anne's computer. The software had come through faster than expected. I didn't really find anything of importance there and felt like I had wasted a morning.

Shortly before lunch, Marcus came back, and we were on our way out when Thibault came in. I retreated to my desk. Marcus asked me to join, but I declined.

While they talked, I quickly grabbed food, bringing something back for my partner.

I didn't expect Thibault pushing me into our interview room, but the way he didn't let me talk was unsurprising. Telling me off like he did took a lot of guts. He had a strength and control that few possessed. And he was right. I shouldn't have kissed him last night. And I should have come clean sooner about Pride. But I hadn't known how to handle it then, and I wasn't any surer on how to handle things now. I needed to move past it and leave it behind me. Deep down, that wasn't what I wanted, but if I repeated it enough to myself, it might stick. Last night had changed things. The feelings he evoked in me still scared me to death, which was fine. I had to concentrate on the case and figure out if Thibault had anything to do with it.

Walking back to my desk, I spotted Marcus in the evidence room adding Thibault's statement and his prints to our list of evidence.

"Hey, Marcus, already done? I have your lunch here. Want to go sit in the conference room and catch up while you eat?"

"Sure, let's go."

Once we were both seated, Marcus gestured for me to go first.

"There wasn't much of anything on Sally Anne's computer. I couldn't find any emails explaining why she was at the duck pond, threats, or anything similar. I contacted her email provider, but they came back with the usual answer of, 'No warrant, no information.' I am making a list so the sergeant or the chief can push warrants for us with a judge. We probably need one for her phone records. It might help us, whether or not we locate her device."

"Good idea. I was a little luckier at the duck pond. The rain didn't damage the scene too much out there as it didn't fall as heavily, thanks to the trees. There was nothing more, but we found the dead buck. A human definitely brought it down."

"Poachers?" I asked.

"I assume so. What leaves me scratching my head is why didn't they take the body? Someone started skinning and cutting it and just left it there."

"This is getting weirder by the second. We need to talk to the park rangers."

Marcus took a bite from his sandwich, then said, "John didn't have much luck last night. It was too dark by the time he arrived at the library. I am going there now to see if I have more luck in the light of day. They are on the same schedule collection as us, Monday and Thursday, so if someone left it in their dumpsters or anywhere on that street, it should still be there."

"What about prints and interviews? When do you want to do those?"

"I asked George to call the members of the Historical Preservation Society, Sally Anne's colleagues, and the library. Apparently, he got into a nasty conversation with none other than Dorothy. She is getting very riled up because we still haven't arrested Thibault. Everybody else is 'too busy' today. They should all come in on Monday or Tuesday, including Dorothy. I am not looking forward to it."

Despite all these years of police work, it still amazed me. People were quick to guess, gossip, and complain when it came to investigations. But ask them to give a bit of their time to help move the inquest forward, and they all scattered like mice seeing the shadow of a cat.

Marcus stood. "Okay, let's go to the library and see what more we can find there. You coming with me this time?"

"Yes, if you don't mind. Dumpster diving is definitely not my definition of a pleasurable time, but I wouldn't mind being outside. And finding her bag might help. At least it would give us some clue of who she was in contact with, her daily life, pictures. And there might be something on it to explain why she was at the duck pond."

Before we could get back to our desks, Mary hollered for us, and we followed her into her lab slash office.

"Hey, guys. It took me longer than I would have liked, but I was able to measure some things through the video. And from what I read in Reginald's report, it concurs."

I nodded, as I had read it before getting started on Sally Anne's computer, but Marcus shook his head. "I am sorry, folks, could you tell me the broad details? I went directly to the duck pond with John this morning and didn't get the chance to look."

"Well, the report says the person who killed Sally Anne did not use a lot of force, and the slash at her throat was not deliberate but more accidental. On any other part of the neck, it would have been insignificant, but it hit the carotid. The angle is straight along her throat, not a downward motion or an upward motion. She was just over five foot five, so someone at least six feet tall would have been able to hit her that way. Someone smaller, like Thibault, would have hit her in the shoulder, or it would have been a downward or upward motion. The man was likely left-handed." She pointed at the screen in front of us and pressed Play.

"Here it is, around 5:00 a.m. The camera is angled for the top of the stairs, but nothing more. A first man comes up. Let's call him P1 for perp number one. He opens the door, and when it sticks, he pulls on it the same way as Thibault, but about four inches higher, maybe. He goes right back down and comes back with a second man. P1 and P2 then go in with Sally Anne. They stay in for about ten minutes. Then they go back out. P2 is taller than P1, and he closes the door with his left hand, same place maybe as P1. Prints on both sides of the door are what you need to focus on. I tried to zoom in, but it's too dark, unfortunately. Even with enhancement and making it brighter, you can't see their faces. I put them in the recognition software, but it quickly came back with Unmatched."

She pressed pause, then clicked on a different icon on her screen. Rubbing her hands, she gushed, "I used this program I love. It enables me to put snippets of the video from different times side by side, so I was able to compare the size of the two men against different people. First is both perps against Thibault." She pressed play, and I almost sighed in relief. Unless Thibault had been slouching on Friday morning, which he hadn't, or he was wearing high heels the night of the murder, he hadn't done it. Neither the killing nor the cover-up. Whether he was being set up remained to be uncovered.

She pressed pause again, then switched on a different video and another two after that. The first one compared me with the men, the second was against Marcus, and the third with John. I was taller than them both, but they were similar to Marcus, so definitely around six feet if not a little smaller.

This helped eliminate suspects. It was definitely no one from the library or the HPS. Most were women. The only two male library employees, Nathaniel and Thibault, were either too small or too tall. Unfortunately, this didn't help us find who had done it. So it was back to hoping the prints would give us something.

"Thanks, Mary." I looked at Marcus. "Well, that eliminates a few people and confirms two people carried her inside."

He nodded. "Yeah, now we just need to find the phone. I really hope we get something out of it."

We left Mary to the rest of her checks. She had put the prints through the system and was working on the footprints to give us a definite shoe size.

We both turned and strode toward our respective desks, fetching our kits and changing into overalls to protect our clothes, and in the direction of the library we went.

**Saturday - Afternoon**

*W*hen we met at the front door, I suggested we go on foot. It would allow us to check the street for cameras, and we could send a list to George as we went so he could call them today or Monday. Businesses were open today, but most would be closed tomorrow. Monday was shaping up to be one busy day.

The police station sat at the entrance of Hampton Street next to the mayor's office, which was a couple of houses down S. Jefferies Boulevard. These two streets, as well as Wichman Street, were the main axes in town and held most businesses. The rest of town was more residential with small mom-and-pop shops here and there. The library was farther down Hampton Street.

On our way, we noticed a camera on an ATM across the street from the Miracle Brew. We didn't see any others. We needed to go door-to-door on Monday to see if anyone had any hidden cameras. Even with an acute angle, you never knew what might show in the reflections. Or so Mary had told me repeatedly.

We arrived at the library, where it looked like nothing was disturbed. The garbage cans, stacked at the back, were small. The library didn't have as much trash as most other businesses. We each took on a trash can and, after placing a tarp on the floor, emptied them. At first glance, I couldn't see anything of interest. Rummaging around, I found a bloody rag.

"Hey, Marcus, can you pass me the bag?" He gave it to me. I pulled out the camera, and after taking pictures of the rag, I placed it in an evidence bag and left it on the tarp. I picked through the rest some more. There was nothing: no phone, wallet, handbag, or keys.

Glancing at Marcus, he shook his head. "What did you find, J?"

"A bloody rag." He quirked a brow, which seemed to be his dominant form of communication these days. "I do mean blood, Marcus. All right, let's pack it up. What do you want to do next?"

Marcus appeared puzzled. "Why are you asking me?"

"Because yesterday we said you were the one leading, didn't we?"

"Yeah, but now we know Thibault had nothing to do with this. I thought you might want to take the lead back."

"No, that's fine. Let's not switch in the middle. We are both going to get confused, and the chief might ask questions I don't want to answer."

Marcus shrugged. "Fine by me. I want to canvass the back streets here and check for easily accessible garbage cans where someone could stash a bag. We got Sally Anne's number from Dorothy yesterday, so provided the phone is not dead, we might hear it."

"Sounds good. Let's go."

Starting from the library, we walked in squares. There weren't many trash cans, and none contained a handbag or ringing phone. Wherever it was, it was definitely ringing. Pity it wasn't anywhere near us. Just as we had given up and were going back toward the station, someone called out to us. "Jack, Marcus." Jessica and Tabitha were coming toward us holding a handbag wrapped in a tea towel.

"Tabitha found this in my "special collection" box. We rarely get this type of item, and we put it away to look at later in the morning as we were checking inventory. It started ringing off the hook. I was going to open it when I realized it wasn't my handbag. Sometimes people forget items in the things they leave for me, but I had a weird feeling, and when I saw you out here, well..." She trailed off.

We approached and asked them to show us the box. Tabitha then placed the handbag on top. One more time, Marcus called Sally Anne's number. The purse started ringing and vibrating. No wonder we'd heard nothing. Brilliant. Thank god the two of them were used to caring for delicate objects. There might still be a couple of handprints, but I wouldn't hold my breath. We took pictures of the box and the bag, then opened it. It held Sally Anne's phone, her wallet, and some knickknacks, but no sign of her keys.

We thanked them and were about to leave when Jessica grabbed my arm. "Jack, not so fast, honey. About that coffee, why not Tuesday? One woman from church would love to meet Thibault."

Both Marcus and Tabitha rolled their eyes, snickering. I had known Tabitha almost as long as Jessica. Tabitha had married Bobby, her high school sweetheart and my best friend, right after college. When I came back to town and started hanging out with them and Marcus again, not that we'd ever lost contact, I discovered I had a lot more in common with the sweet brunette than I'd thought possible.

To bring my attention back to her, Jessica squeezed my arm, and I extracted myself from her clutches, taking a step back. "I am sorry, Jessica. It seems I wasn't clear enough yesterday. I am not interested. I know my mother keeps telling you it will happen, but it won't. In case you didn't hear it fifteen years ago or still don't get it, I am gay. I am interested in men and men only. I won't put myself in a closet or live a life that is not for me simply because of what you or my mother wishes for.

"The moment I was outed, though the worst time of my life, was the most liberating too. So no, I won't have coffee with you on Tuesday or any other day, and I certainly won't be your date to any ball or soiree or social function you might be going to. Ever. Thank you for the handbag. This is great for our case. Have a good day."

On that, I turned on my heels, kissed Tabitha's cheek, grabbed Marcus and the handbag, and left.

Before Marcus could speak, I stopped him. "I know you probably want to comment on what just happened, but not right now, Marcus. Put it in the same box of 'Confessions by Jack' where you put the one from yesterday, and let's concentrate on what we are doing, okay?"

He nodded. We walked back to the station and went straight to the evidence locker. It felt a lot like déjà vu, except this time we were lucky to have her handbag with us. I had high hopes for the handbag and her phone. The battery was low, so we needed a charger, but that wouldn't be a problem.

Once we added the extra items to the log, Marcus turned to me and suggested, "Why don't we do one last sweep of the library to ensure we missed nothing yesterday? We took prints on top of surfaces, like the desk, tables, etc. But we didn't dust underneath. Remember that article we read on how suspects think of removing prints from obvious places, but not from places they would unconsciously touch?"

"Yes, superb idea. Let's go."

We trotted back to the library. Though I'm sure the idea had occurred to Marcus earlier, if we had started here, we wouldn't have found the handbag until at least Monday if not later. Jessica and Tabitha had probably had the handbag since Friday morning, and only because it had rung did they remember to look inside. God knows how long it might have been forgotten, otherwise. I was happy to walk back and forth to the library if it meant more clues coming our way.

Once there, we walked to the side entrance. Nothing seemed disturbed. The tape was unmoved from the door. We opened it, and as expected, it stuck.

"Wait, you took prints all over, right?"

"Yes, I took prints at Thibault's level."

"Did you do higher? Or further?"

Marcus frowned, thinking back. "I definitely did above and below. Why?"

"From what Mary showed us, the perps are taller than Thibault, right?"

He nodded.

"His arms are shorter as well, and we don't all pull the same way, do we? I couldn't quite see how they pulled on the video, as their body was blocking the camera. How do you open a door when it's stuck?"

He smiled. "I use my elbow."

"Your elbow? How do you pull with your elbow, you weirdo?"

"Simple. I put my elbow against the door and push. That's usually when my hands are busy. How do you open it?"

"It depends. I either simply pull, like Thibault did yesterday, or if I don't want to bang the door and make noise or marks on the wall, I put my hand on the door with my fingers to the outside, leveraging my elbow against the door frame. Then I push."

"Huh. You think you know a guy, and then you discover his weird door-opening habits." We snickered.

We both pulled on gloves, and placing my hands where we knew Thibault had pulled yesterday, I opened the door half-way. Marcus applied powder to the inside, while I did the outside and edges. Using my stuck-door method, my thumb would fall to the side of the door, not the outside. We found prints on both sides we hadn't collected the day before. After putting stickers on the door, we took pictures before lifting the prints and carefully stacking them in the box.

We then went inside the employee room. Though we had done the floor yesterday, Marcus still dusted one chair with powder. "What are you doing?" I asked.

"This chair is away from the table. One of the library employees might not have pushed it back, but..." Made sense. Suspect Everything was one of the first things we'd learned.

He lifted a few partial prints, most likely from the employees of the library. If we didn't have anyone to match them to, prints weren't going to lead us anywhere. I would keep my fingers crossed that the interviews on Monday would bring some answers.

Marcus finished taking pictures and prints, then gazed at me with a smile. "Feel like role-playing with me?" I smirked. We had both loved that when we were kids. The best thing was sleeping at Marcus's growing up and playing D&D with two other friends. On occasion we would don costumes in his room and pretend to be one character or another. When we were teenagers, his mom brought us to a couple of live role plays as birthday presents, and we'd had a blast. We didn't get the chance to do it much anymore, maybe once a year for Pride, and we rarely went full cosplay anymore. If my parents had let me be, I would have been quite the nerd. Things being as they were, they'd pushed me into farming and sports.

"Sure, where do we start from?" I asked.

"Let's go back out. From what Doc said yesterday, they left her somewhere, probably in a car, before moving her to the library. Let's assume there were two people." We moved outside. He placed me in the lot, then jogged to the door, acted as if opening it, and came back down where we both mimicked lifting a body. It would be better if we had a mannequin or something to simulate the weight and size. "Wait a second. Let me run to the fire station. I'll see if I can borrow their training doll." With a snort, Marcus nodded.

I rushed down the street at a trot, happy to discover they weren't on a call.

"Hey, Jack!" and "What's up, Detective?" greeted me.

"Hey guys, where is your captain? Could I borrow the mannequin by any chance?"

"Need a hot date, Jack? I know a couple of people here who would love to volunteer as tribute." I scowled, then laughed at the look of horror on a few men's faces. Yeah, police or fire departments were not the most open-minded places out there. Bobby didn't care, though, and usually liked to stir the pot. I knew exactly who he was referring to.

"Are you volunteering, Bobby? I am not sure Tabitha would appreciate..."

He chuckled. "Newbie, go grab the doll for the detective." A couple minutes later, the young man came back with it.

I thanked him, then turning to the men at large, said, "Thanks, guys. I'll bring it back once we are done at the library."

That thing was heavy. I turned around, lifting it, and

started walking back. I hadn't made it ten feet from the station when the doll's weight was lifted as Bobby picked up the bottom.

"Sorry, man. I realized what you meant to use this for when you said library, and I know how much that shit weighs. If you're gonna do what I believe, it will grow heavy by the time you get there, and you won't have the strength to do too much more."

"Thanks, Bobby. I appreciate it. That's so sweet of you," I simpered, batting my eyelashes.

"Oh, don't go throwing hearts at me, baby. As you pointed out, my wife wouldn't appreciate."

I snorted. His wife would play right along with me. "No, you're right. It would disappoint her to not get a piece of this." I flexed my muscles.

Still ribbing each other, we arrived at the library. He waved, shouting hello to Marcus, and ran back to the station. I took a breather and stretched my arms. I wouldn't need to do arms tonight at the gym. Fiddlesticks, that had been heavy. I almost regretted suggesting this to Marcus. We both grabbed the doll. Marcus started walking backward slowly up the stairs. Wobbling a little, he grabbed the railing. We looked at each other.

"You did that yesterday, didn't you?"

"Yeah, I did. Why?"

"Did you dust under?" I looked pointedly at how he held the bar.

He shook his head and laughed. "Nope."

"Okay, let's take a mental note of this and do it on our way out."

We moved forward. Since we'd forgotten to switch on the light, he was navigating slowly. Marcus dropped the mannequin. Going to flip the switch, he stopped dead in his tracks. He pulled out his kit and powdered around the light switch and wall. He placed markers and the lifting paper, leaving it all there.

We picked the mannequin back up and progressed in the dark, stumbling in the corridor. The sun filtered into the primary room, which gave us a bit of light to go toward the front desk. We didn't encounter anything else. We tried lifting the doll to place her on the desk, but it wasn't that simple, so I left Marcus holding it on his side and went around. Once there, I helped him lift it on the table. We dusted the entire place for prints and didn't stumble on any other surfaces in between.

At least we'd covered most of it, which was great. We should be able to release the crime scene today. There wasn't much more we could retrieve. Heading back to the employee lounge, we lifted the prints on the light switch. We then turned on the lights and examined the front room. Once done, we grabbed the doll and shuffled back to the side entrance. We locked it, then went down the stairs. There, we did the railing on both sides, bottom part only.

We packed up everything and placed the box on top of the doll, each awkwardly holding on and hoping we wouldn't drop anything. On our way to the police department, we left the doll at the fire station. They had left on a call, so we wrote a note on a Post-it and placed it on the doll, thanking them again.

Once at the station, we walked straight to the evidence room. It was already 4:00 p.m., but since we had a couple of hours left before the day was done, Marcus suggested we review some of the evidence, the phone in particular.

We retrieved the handbag from the evidence box, having left the phone there. When we tried to switch it on, it died on us. No more battery. Of course. We checked the make and model. Marcus went to ask our colleagues if anyone had a charger while I called the phone store to see if they carried any. They did, so I rushed over.

Back at the station with a charger, I plugged the phone in. We would need a few minutes to get it started, and with how our luck was running, it was likely password protected. Our great unlock program would be useful. Marcus was more versed in technology, so I left the phone and started on the evidence.

Mary was working on the shoe prints still and hadn't had any luck yet. She confirmed the size of the imprint from the library was a size ten. Most of Thibault's shoes were a size eight or eight and a half. She had started on the fingerprints, but the network had died on her, so I took over scanning them for her.

Marcus came back into the room. "I talked to Charlene and told her we were done with the scene. She will go in tomorrow to assess what needs to be cleaned and call the number I gave her. I told her we were keeping the key, and if we need to check something out, we will let her know."

"Great. In the meantime, I got a charger from the store. I plugged it in already, so you just need to hook it up to your program or whatever magic you do with locked phones," I told him. He snorted. I wasn't a techno snob or technophobe by any means, but technology had never been my friend.

While I kept going with my scanning, he started the other computer and connected the phone to it. We would leave it there as long as it took for it to unlock, which could be anywhere from a couple of minutes to seventy-two hours, depending on how good her password or lock was. Or so Marcus told me. Once I was done with my very boring task, I connected to the server and searched for the prints.

Marcus's evidence held one more set I hadn't noticed—

Thibault's prints. I scanned these in as well and plugged them into the system. The program would do two things: check Thibault's prints against those taken at the scene and check the scene prints against everyone in the system. As we now knew he didn't do it, the first check would help eliminate his prints from the crime scene. The second one would take a few days if it even found a match.

I stretched, placed all the prints back into the evidence boxes, and put them away. I was done for the day. Thank god tomorrow was Sunday.

We went back to our desks, grabbed our stuff, and left. As I was about to go to my truck, Marcus stopped me. "Hey, J, how about a drink at the Tavern? I need to shower the day away, so how about seven p.m.? I'll even buy some food."

Ready to say no, I opened my mouth, but what came out was the opposite. "Sounds good. Especially the food. Make it seven thirty and I'll be there."

We parted ways then. As it was just a little after six, once home, I went for a run, showered, and walked to the Tavern.

**Saturday - evening**

On my way home, I thought over what we had bought the night before and detoured by the store. Tomorrow was market day, and I needed stuff to make sandwiches for myself. I would make some for Sam too. He had a stand but almost always forgot to bring himself something to eat. It had become a habit of mine. Whether or not I would exhibit, I would bring him lunch. If one of his guys were there, we would break together and walk around the market. Otherwise, we would simply eat at his stand between customers.

After my shopping, I went back home. Putting away the groceries reminded me of the previous day. I was glad Jack hadn't ever set foot in the house before last night. The impact that one moment in time had had on me was significant already. If we had been friendlier over the past two years and regularly stayed at each other's places, I couldn't imagine what would have happened. He might not have jumped to such conclusions. And last night wouldn't have gone so badly. I couldn't bring myself to regret this.

Now that I knew Jack and Mystery Man were the same, I needed to either move on like Sam had urged me to last year or move past my hurt. Neither would be easy. My more rational brain understood why he jumped to such conclusions. As we didn't know each other much, asking him to trust me was, in a way, a big leap. After all, cops were taught to question everything and not take people at their word. Even my small foray in criminology had made me more suspicious.

My heart was bruised. I had gone with the idea everyone always hammered on everyone else with: to be happy, you needed to be two. I wasn't able to move on from Mystery Man last year, and chances were high I wouldn't get past Jack and last night anytime soon. I had tried to find someone else. I'd had hookups. None of it had worked.

But if you were unhappy on your own, how could you be happy with someone else? Some self-love was in order—get your mind out of the gutter. Whether it lasted a week or a few years, it didn't matter. My mam always told me, "Love yourself, and others will fall in love with you too." She said to be comfortable with someone, you needed to find comfort in your own company. That's what she did before she met my father. I wouldn't close myself off to anything coming my way, but I wouldn't go looking for it anymore. Navigating through other people's expectations would be harder, but life was like that. Make decisions for yourself and then justify them ad nauseam to all and sundry.

If something were to happen with Jack, then it would come back around once things cooled down a bit.

Once I was done tidying up the kitchen, I went upstairs and threw on comfy clothes, then went back outside where I spent most of the afternoon taking care of my garden, weeding, watering, and preparing the beds for my seedlings. I brushed my animals so they would be presentable the next day. Taking them all to the market would be too much hassle. So I switched, depending on who was the most relaxed. I had learned the hard way animals had their own minds, and if they weren't into it, you'd better be prepared to pay the consequences, literally and figuratively.

A pissed-off Arthur, one of my miniature goats, running through the market with a child on his back, slamming through tables and people came to mind. I shuddered.

After cleaning myself up, I threw on a pair of tight black jeans and a cropped T-shirt that said, "Relax, I am here" in bold pink on black. I put on some black eyeliner, brushed my hair, and put it into a proper bun at the top. I hadn't shaved in a few days, and dark stubble completed the overall look.

I checked my phone to see if I had any messages, but I'd never restarted it, so the network was still "Not Found." Switching it back on, I noticed a text from my mam, one from Sam, and one from Charlene. Merde. I'd forgotten to call to cancel my Skype session with my mam today. I sent her a quick reply to reassure her I wasn't dead like she'd accused and told her I would call her the following week. I definitely wasn't ready to talk to her. Charlene's text was simply to let me know the crime scene at the library was released, she'd left the box of books for tomorrow in our break room, and cleaners would come in the next day to tidy up the library.

I let Sam know I was on my way and jumped into my car.

I parked at the library and rushed to the back door. I didn't want to go in, but removing the Band-Aid now would be better. Not pausing to think, I unlocked the door and went in. My first step inside had me shuddering. My skin crawled. I switched on the light and saw the box on the nearest table. Thank god. I picked it up and hurried back out, barely remembering the light. Once the door was locked, I leaned against it and sent a text to Charlene to let her know I'd picked up the books. If this was my reaction now, I needed to arrive early on Monday to take baby steps back inside.

I dropped the books in the car and walked to the Tavern. It was a lovely old building on the outside, with red brick walls and small windows, and the inside was inviting and cozy. All black wood with white fabrics on the chairs, benches, and stools to lighten it up. Local bands often came in on Friday and Sunday nights. And Saturday was when you could get your groove on. We were early enough to hear each other without yelling.

Sam and George were already seated in a booth at the back. The speakers were facing the other way, which would make it even easier to talk. Once I greeted them, we ordered some food and drinks.

"So," George started, "what happened yesterday?"

Sam laughed, and I groaned. I told them everything after finding Sally Anne's body including my disastrous morning and my epiphany on Mystery Man.

My statement was met with joint expressions of disbelief.

"What?"

"No way!"

"Oh, yes way. I still don't know how to process this. I guess you were both wrong. Mystery Man was right in front of me this whole time, just not in Charleston like I believed," I told them.

"God, this is a lot to unpack, sweetie." Sam patted my hand.

George nodded beside him. "Can you forgive him? I mean, it's his job, after all. I have heard the officers, including Jack and Marcus, complaining often enough about it. I mean, our town is getting bigger every year, so they don't often have to arrest or suspect someone they know anymore, but a few years back, when I first started, at least once a week, they brought in someone I was familiar with. They were never happy about it. If people didn't forgive them or keep trusting in them, we would be in big trouble by now." George raised a hand. "I am not excusing him. I am just saying maybe cut him some slack."

"Cut him some slack?" Sam exclaimed. "Are you kidding? This is not something you can forgive, George. He accused him of murdering Sally Anne."

"He didn't," George countered. "Jack said he suspected him, which is a big difference. He didn't arrest him or even interrogate him. I am guessing his brief foray into Thibault's shoes was more of a..."

I cut him off. "A stupid move on his part which could have cost him his job. In any case, I need to take a step back. I am not ready to forgive anything. I don't even know if I can trust him not to turn things back around on me. And he is still investigating the murder, with me as their prime suspect."

Our food arrived, but before we dug in, George added, "Jack took a step back on the investigation and is letting Marcus lead this time. Mary told me Jack looked relieved when she told them the evidence was definitely pointing away from you."

I chewed thoughtfully; I was about to ask what evidence when someone spoke in the booth behind me and I froze. George and Sam both perked up and put their fingers to their mouths. I shook my head, but their frantic hand gestures made me stay put.

**Jack**

When I arrived at the Tavern, Marcus was already seated in a booth at the back. It was darker, but we wouldn't need to shout at each other. I stopped at the bar and ordered a dark beer. We would see about food later. Right now I needed to relax. Marcus thought the same, and we sipped our beer in silence after greeting each other.

"So," he began, more hesitant than I had ever seen him. "You ready to talk to me or are we going to ignore everything and move on?"

"What do you mean?"

"Don't play coy with me, Tomlins. Yesterday you were so sure Thibault had done it when we were at the crime scene. You wouldn't listen when I talked. You left more cheerful than I have seen you in a while and arrived this morning grumpier than a bear with a sore paw. I learned through the grapevine you were shopping and went home with Thibault. Today you let me lead. Now we learned Thibault didn't do it, and you looked happy, devastated, and relieved. To say nothing of the look on your face when you both left the room at the precinct this afternoon. So spill. You're not getting out of it this time."

When he started talking about Thibault, I was staring at my beer. I blinked a few times. I didn't know where to start.

"When Ruth died, Thibault inherited her house, her animals, everything. We had talked about it before it happened, and I told her I didn't want any of it." I raised a hand. "Don't start. It was not because of some sense of sacrifice or whatnot—it was self-preservation. First, I didn't want to hear all the whispers, gossip, et cetera. Second, I didn't want her family suing me for anything. And last but not least, I wouldn't want to live there on my own with her memories. I would miss her and David far too much, and I would end up selling it or leaving and then regretting it.

"When I saw Thibault the first time, it was a shock. I know people thought I disliked him on sight because he got Ruth's house or was gay. Or a mix of the two or whatever else they could think of. But that's far from the truth. Hell, I had been helping Ruth answer his mother's letters for a few years. I even met Helene a few times, and I adored her. I still do. I imagined him much younger than he was. Seeing him here, all grown up and handsome and sweet, was a punch to the gut. The fact that he had Ruthy's smile and hair didn't help any.

"So, yeah, at first I stayed away, stuck in my grief, feeling sorry for myself and unable to go to the one place that had been my refuge for so many years. I could have befriended him, asked him if I could go see the animals anytime I needed. But somehow, it didn't feel right. My crazy attraction to him definitely didn't help.

"So I became more and more rude, trying to push him away, but it backfired big time because all it did was make him snarkier with me, and you know I have something for snarky men. It all culminated last year when we went to Charleston for Pride."

Marcus's sharp intake of breath told me he definitely hadn't seen that one coming.

I finished my beer in one gulp. "I am not pausing for the suspense. If I am going to continue, then I need more to drink. And food. What do you want? I am going for the chicken wings, the loaded cheese fries, and the shrimp and grits. Wanna share?"

"Sure do. Get me a burger. Keep the grits and shrimp to yourself. And get me a refill, will ya?"

I went up to the bar and placed our order, walking back with two beers and a pitcher of lemonade. After all, we were both on call tomorrow, and a hangover definitely wouldn't help if we had to go in.

Once settled, I picked up where I'd left off. I didn't want to reveal too much. Parts of it were far too private to share.

I reminded him how we'd ended up in a bar, in Charleston, dressed up and hiding behind masks. He nodded, waving for me to continue. Our food came, and I chewed on a fry before starting to talk. I explained how my eye got caught on a beautiful man and how I ended up with him in one of the small alcoves. Marcus was a brilliant listener. He always waited to ask questions. And I knew he would have a million soon if I didn't hurry up. The food was a good thing to keep him occupied.

When I reached the part where I was face-to-face with Thibault, he looked stunned. I stopped talking then; there were some things I wanted to keep to myself. But I couldn't help remembering everything.

The smell of sweat and cum, Thibault's sweet taste when he kissed me. The feel of his arms and his strength. His body against mine. The tears I couldn't stop from falling after. It was seared in my mind, and I loved every second of it. It had scared me then, the same way last night's kiss scared me. So much potential lived in both of those kisses. And I had been looking for someone like Thibault for a long time. Maybe too long. I'd gotten used to being single, and I could already hear the gossip and my mother's screeching.

But the way his body had fit mine so perfectly wouldn't leave me. And what I saw behind the snarky facade yesterday was intriguing. I didn't know how to make my brain switch off and try. I definitely needed to apologize and see if he could find it in his heart to forgive me.

Marcus rapped his fist on the table and called my name,

bringing me back to the present. "Whatever you got lost into looked a lot like heaven and a little like hell."

"All right, man, you know I don't dish as much as you do. I spent a sweet moment with him. One of the most magical times of my life."

"Found your unicorn, hm?"

"Unicorn?"

"Yes. It goes like this. We all have needs and wants and unique ideas of what a relationship or even simply a sex partner should be like. We both know if you let go, from a personality perspective, you and Thibault would just click."

I blushed. "Yeah, we do."

"A unicorn is that one person who fits all of your needs and desires. I guess you realized that from a sexual or chemistry point of view, you two click, thanks to your night together. And it made you run scared, am I right?"

"Yeah, yeah, you are. He is most likely my unicorn. Or my lobster." I snorted. The look of disgust on his face told me he knew I was referencing Friends, and he was bracing himself for an entire episode retelling. I threw my napkin at him, which made him grin. Yeah, letting my playful side out felt good.

"Yes, I ran scared. When I saw him again the following week, what did you expect me to say with everyone scrutinizing us at the café? 'Hey, Thibault, I am the guy you hooked up with at Pride.' Yeah, right. As if. One of the first people I saw the next day was my mother. She, of course, caught me off guard, right as I was bracing myself to just go talk to Thibault. You can imagine the type of things she hissed at me. And yes, I was stupid enough to let her voice get into my head every time I saw him."

Marcus clasped his hand around mine. I could feel some stares and didn't care. Once I was outed and Marcus came out as bi a few years later, rumors swirled around us, especially once I came back to town. People thought we were together. Apart from a couple of youthful kisses and caresses, nothing had ever really happened. Our friendship felt too important. And as we grew older, we felt more like brothers. When we reunited the first time on a break from college, we kissed, thinking, *Why not? Why not if it was that easy?* We both recoiled, laughing. There was no chemistry.

The one thing I had been thankful for was how no one suspected anything when we were teenagers. The fact that I was a rich white boy and he was a black boy had often created issues already. With my parents especially. If people had known about our sexual identities when we were teens, I am sure things would have gone badly. Since we were now both law enforcement and muscular men, people did not comment, but bigots and racists were everywhere, and I knew it wasn't easy for Marcus.

I squeezed his hand, and we both grabbed our glasses, smirking over the rim. God only knew what rumors would run around town tomorrow. Did you hear? Marcus swooped in and staked a claim back on his partner. *I wonder what the little librarian must be thinking.*

"So what happened yesterday, then?"

"We talked, really talked. About my relationship with Ruth, my parents, expectations. He fell asleep on my shoulder. He woke up when one of the cats jumped off of the couch or whatever. He was so close and a little rumpled from sleep. So I leaned in and kissed him. And it felt so, so right. But my mother, of all people, called and I picked up thinking it was the station."

He interrupted me. "I have told you countless times to give her a distinct ringtone. Give me your phone. Now, Jack."

I complied, unlocking it and passing it on to him. "Don't do anything silly."

He waved me off. "Come on, I am past that age." As if. "I promise I won't send anything to anyone. Now, I guess you ran scared again. But what happened to make you both so mad this morning and him so close to calling his lawyer?"

"I am an idiot when it comes to him. Once I hung up with my mom, I told him I was going to bed and ran upstairs. He'd switched the bedroom and the guest room, and in my rush, I didn't ask and went straight into the room I used to sleep in. Well, imagine my surprise when fifteen minutes later, the bed was full of cat, dog, and Thibault because it's his bedroom now. The next morning, he found me rummaging in his closet and then taking pictures of the soles of his shoes while he was in the shower."

Marcus laughed so hard he cried. "You are right—you are an idiot. Why would you do something so stupid?"

"I don't know. I panicked. Between seeing Jessica at the grocery store, my mother, that kiss that reminded me of the potential between us, and our murder investigation painting him as a potential suspect, I got scared. Hell, I have been for the past two years. I know I could fall hard and fast for a man like him. Scratch that—for him, period.

"But we will be under scrutiny. Yes, a few LGBTQ people live here now, but apart from two preexisting relationships from before people settled here, most of us are single. Thanks to my mother, everything I do is scrutinized and discussed. I don't want to put that kind of pressure on us. What happens if it doesn't work out?"

"God, Jack, you ask yourself far too many questions. You could have tried being friends. Hell, I did. Now we know he's not a suspect, what are you going to do?"

I shrugged. Yes, the idea of being friends had crossed my

mind, but when I saw the gossip swirling around town over my friendship with Marcus or Thibault's friendship with George and Sam, I wasn't sure I wanted that kind of scrutiny. Things were complicated enough.

We had finished our dinner in contemplative silence, nursing our beers, when I noticed the booth behind Marcus leaving. Sam and George waved at me and started walking away. Thibault stared at me. I wasn't sure what to do or say.

Marcus cleared his throat, "Sorry, man. I didn't see you were having a staring contest with Thibault."

"Did you know they were here?" I asked him.

"What? No. I wouldn't set you up. Though I don't think him hearing all this was bad."

"Yeah, well, we will see. I don't see how it could help either."

"Don't overthink this, Jack. Give it a few days. Still want to go to the market with me tomorrow?"

"Sure, why not? If you don't mind, I think I am going to go home now. I feel like this week is never-ending."

Marcus laughed. "No worries, my friend. I am going to follow suit."

**15**

---

THIBAULT

**Sunday, April 14, 2019**

*S*unday morning Lady Gaga woke me up early—too early—and I so wanted to sleep in. Last night had been rather hard, despite falling asleep easily enough. I had awoken a few times, either from nightmares or from trying to grab onto Jack, only to find he wasn't there. Stupid detective. Stupid murder. Cranky was my name today.

The conversation we had eavesdropped on did not help me move on. I knew Jack was a complex man, and his gruff exterior could be a sort of defense mechanism. Last night proved me right, but what to do with the information was still a puzzle to me. Marcus's unicorn theory wasn't far from the truth. Jack pushed all my buttons. But now that I knew who exactly he was and our amazing chemistry, did I want to throw it away over a stupid mistake or did I want to explore it?

I shook my head and stood. It was far too early for the type of deep thoughts I needed to sort through all this. I dressed for market. Nothing fancy, as I had to take part of the zoo with me, but a brown shirt, perfect to hide stains, and an old pair of jeans would do.

I trudged down the stairs to look over the animals. I fed all of them, then checked on their mood, hoping theirs was better than mine. Judging an animal's feelings was simple: Come around with the lead, cage, leash, or whatever, signifying you were going on a ride. If they stayed there looking at you or acting indifferent, then they were coming with you. If they ran off, hissed, or kicked, they definitely weren't coming.

So today I got Tipsy, one of my Silkie hens, and Silky, my Kadaknath hen. Betsy the pig and Marylin the dwarf goat were coming too. And once I had loaded everyone and was about to start, I noticed two stowaways, Smokey and Skye, my Himalayan cat and Australian Shepherd. They didn't always come, but nine times out of ten they would. They either rode in the trailer with the rest of the animals or jumped in front, depending on who was along.

Today they were both in front. I double-checked the food and water for all of them as well as my own, piled next to the box of books, then set out for the market. I loved market day. In the beginning, it was hard but now it felt natural. Waking up so early on a Sunday was a pain, but seeing the faces of people of all ages at the sight of my little zoo warmed my heart every time.

A month after I arrived in town, we had a council of war. The city, despite having a bigger budget thanks to its growth, was thinking of closing the library. We settled on two initiatives: daily book clubs and readings for children, teenagers, and adults and the booth at the market twice a month. That had been my idea, but without the zoo. That had been Gwendolyn's idea and had scared me to death at first. A couple of mishaps and two years later, it was one of the highlights of my week.

When I arrived, my stall was ready for me. It was more of a little paddock with a small plastic swimming pool I would fill with water and mud for Betsy, as well as a few bales of straw. Tipsy and Silky didn't care as long as they could perch on their cases, and Marylin would probably run around, jump on tables, and such. I placed everyone in their enclosure, then set up the booth with the box I picked up the night before from the library.

As I finished, Sam came my way with what looked like a steaming cup of coffee in his hands. That man was my savior. "Thank god for you and your delicious nectar." We both snorted. An elderly lady glowered at us for a second before moving on, snickering.

Glad I could amuse someone with my half-awake thoughts.

"Hey, sweetie. How are you doing today?"

"Good, you?"

"All set and ready for the hordes to descend. I can't wait to see what goodies some of the antique shops will have for show today. And the gossip. Market day is the best."

"Yes, sounds good. We still on for lunch later, Sam? I have your sandwiches with me."

"If it wasn't for our lack of chemistry, I would marry you on the spot."

I laughed. "I'll see you at your booth later, future husband."

Shaking my head, I went back to my space. I wasn't sure what I would do without Sam and George.

The morning started easy enough. I had the feeling it wouldn't last. A few early risers stopped by, regulars at the booth. They didn't always get the opportunity to come to the library, so this was perfect for them to bring books back to us and pick up fresh ones. We tried to have a diverse selection, especially for these sorts of people.

Next were a few harried parents with toddlers. While the kids petted the animals, they looked at the books. I had the friendliest of the bunch today, so I didn't worry too much but kept as close an eye as possible. The best thing was Skye. She was great at inserting herself between an animal and child if she sensed danger for either. And her quiet woof signaled something was afoot, alerting me.

After the first wave, more people arrived, and I was glad to see my dark angel Reagan. She was sixteen, a total nerd with an edgy look, almost goth. She hated it when I called her my dark angel, but I couldn't help it. She was working part-time at the library, and I loved having her there. Her voice was amazing, and she was wonderful with the kids. She would often join me on Sundays, but never early, god forbid.

When the church let out, I sensed more looks coming my way—well, stares. It was a little unsettling. Then came Dorothy. I didn't notice her at first, busy helping an elderly gentleman find his next book.

Her shrieked "Murderer!" startled us both.

She was almost foaming at the mouth. A few church ladies and fellow members of the HPS were with her. It reminded me of a few other occasions when they had cornered me at my booth, usually with Sally Anne in the lead. There were two stark differences: the absence of Sally Anne and the other ladies, all sneering at me, stayed back.

"I am sorry?" I spluttered. "Can I help you with something?"

The sound coming out of her mouth next sounded like a war cry. She rushed toward my booth, finger pointed straight at my face.

"You should be ashamed of yourself. Showing up like nothing happened. This is a travesty, you still walking free. I have told the police, and I'll go directly to the mayor tomorrow. You should be in jail for what you did to Sally Anne. Rubbing our faces in your sinful ways, parading with one man after the other. Disgraceful. You should be behind bars." What had started in a shriek ended in a snarl.

I almost took a step back, the stares burning a hole through me. Whatever I said wouldn't help me, in her eyes or the ones of the people gawking at us. If I apologized, she would take it as an admission of guilt. If I claimed innocence, she would throw it back in my face.

Reagan took a deep breath beside me as if ready to launch into battle, but I stopped her, placing my hand on her arm and shaking my head slightly.

"You have nothing to say? You will burn in hell for your sins and doing this to Sally Anne. You will see. The reckoning is near. Soon people will see through your lies, your niceties and platitudes. You will get what you deserve."

She slammed her fist on the pile of books closest to her and shouted, "Murderer!"

"That is enough, Dorothy," a deep voice I was starting to equally love and loathe growled. "What do you think you are doing?"

"Ah, Detective Tomlins. Finally here to do your job and arrest this man?" she sneered. At seeing Jack, a triumphant look quickly replaced the disgust on her face.

"Nope," Marcus replied. "I don't think so. As we told you already twice, Thibault had nothing to do with it, apart from finding the body."

She squared her shoulders and whirled toward Marcus. "Lies. You are caught in his web of deceit."

Jack cut her off. "No, we are not, but you are clouded by grief. I am, once again, very sorry for your loss, but evidence retrieved at the scene proves it wasn't Thibault."

She deflated as Jack's words stole the wind right out of her sails.

Her friends rushed over, and after spitting "Sinner" and "Shame on you," they ushered Dorothy away.

Marcus came around the stall, gave me a hug, and then moved toward Sam's coffee stall, calling over his shoulder, "Want anything apart from coffee, Jack?"

"Yes, a scone, please," was all Jack said before coming close to me. He gestured for me to move to the side, and Reagan stepped forward to man the booth.

"Are you all right?" Jack murmured.

"I have been better. Thank you for this. You didn't have to. I don't want you to get into trouble by saying things that aren't true. Or that you don't believe."

He looked taken aback. "What?"

"Well, you're the one who took pictures of my shoes, aren't you?"

He blushed. Since I had noticed it once, it was easier to catch. "I am sorry. You can't know how sorry I feel."

"That you got caught?"

"No," he grumbled. "That I did such a stupid thing. I know it excuses nothing, but I was looking for something to put a barrier between us."

"You are right." He looked hopeful until I added, "It doesn't excuse anything. It's easy to say. I wish instead of pulling a dumb stunt, you would have talked to me like a rational adult. Shite, I would have taken a simple 'I am not interested' or 'It's too complicated.' What hurts the most was you were convinced I was guilty. Probably still are."

"I wasn't, not really. And I am definitely not anymore. I used it as a reason to not get close to you. I would have happily kissed you all night. And most likely let things progress much further."

A throat clearing behind us made him stop. Reagan trying to be subtle, which she wasn't known for, reminded us both we were in public. And apparently, we hadn't been quiet, if the way people looked at us was any indication.

"Let me know if she gives you any more grief. Like I told her, we have evidence proving you had nothing to do with it." Jack handed me a paper with his number on it. He left, meeting with Marcus at the coffee stall.

After Dorothy and Jack, I hoped the rest of the morning would go faster and with no more interruptions. I wasn't sure I could take more of this.

People came and went, some trying to talk about Sally Anne and Dorothy and some wanting details about my relationship with Jack. Reagan was quick to shut them all down. I was even more grateful than usual for her to be there with me. Of the three women working at the library, she had the biggest temper, but it came out as cold and cutting. I was impressed a sixteen-year-old could make people three times her age almost cower in fear with a simple look and a couple of words.

"You need to teach me how you do that," I told her during one of the rare lulls.

"Teach you what?" she asked, eyebrow raised.

I waved my hand, encompassing her. "This. Your way of shutting down people so efficiently. I either ramble, get mad, or break down."

She snorted. "Yeah, I noticed. Not sure how you survived to thirty-five."

"Hey, you take that back. I am not even thirty yet."

Shrugging, she smiled. "Sorry, you old people all look the same to me."

I laughed. "Thank you, you cheeky minx. I am happy you were here with me today."

"The day is not over yet. You don't know my secret plans for after we pack this up, my friend."

I paused. Hm.

Our next customers interrupted us. Tom and a man I didn't know approached the booth, so I left Reagan to care for the mom with two preteens.

I had always liked Tom. Unlike the other people at his church, he had always been friendly. I'd always sensed something was different about him. My gaydar wasn't one hundred percent accurate, and in his case, it was probably wrong. But he pinged, hard. If he was gay or bi, I couldn't really blame him for keeping it to himself. Though I knew it was none of my business, I couldn't help feeling sorry for him. I hadn't stayed long in the closet, as I was outed when I was seventeen. But I knew the fear of discovery and wondering what people would think. If things would change.

It wasn't my place to say anything. On more than one occasion, I'd hinted we could talk. I wasn't sure if Tom hadn't gotten the message, thought I was coming on to him and wasn't interested (which definitely wasn't the goal—he was cute but not for me), or if he simply didn't want to.

From what I had seen of his church, they definitely weren't the openminded bunch they boasted themselves to be. Quite the contrary. Don't tell me you're openminded and "Love thy neighbor" and all that shite if you would then throw women at me right, left, and center so I could walk the path of redemption and stop my sinful ways. As if it was a choice. Get on the first woman you find, and boom, it cures you.

I had stopped that crap as early on as I could. But two years later, they still tried.

As his parents were still part of the congregation, I knew Jack had grown up in that church and their beliefs. And what

I'd heard in the past forty-eight hours showed he could never shake off the things they believed in.

Ah well. I was happy to see Tom. It would be a nice change.

"Hey Tom, my man. How are you doing?" Did that sound far too enthusiastic? Yeah, probably.

"Good morning, Thibault. I am doing just fine today. How are you?" He looked uncomfortable. Probably heard Dorothy and her cronies at church before coming here. I hoped Jack telling her off would soon do the rounds too, so people officially knew I had nothing to do with Sally Anne's murder.

"I am all right. Could have been a better day. How are you holding up? With everything?"

"What everything? It has been business as usual since last time we met." He gave the weirdest chuckle.

"I am talking about Sally Anne, silly. You were part of the same church group, weren't you? I am really sorry for your loss. I saw a few people from her church and the HPS today, and they all seemed pretty distraught. I assumed it was the same for you." Distraught was one way to put it.

Smokey wrapped herself around my legs. Then once I had her in my arms, she climbed on top of me and draped herself over my shoulders. Her weight was comforting.

"It was quite a shock. Church today was... sad. The minister gave a beautiful speech. Sally Anne's niece is not here yet, so we won't have the funeral until she can make it. But I didn't know Sally Anne well. This is my friend Jason." He introduced the man with him. He seemed to be the same age as Tom, same height but bulkier. "He was here when I learned of her death, so he has helped keep my mind off things."

I shook hands with Jason. "Hi, Jason. I am Thibault. What brings you to town? Apart from keeping our sweet Tom here company?"

"Nice to meet you. I try to come around twice a year to see Tom, and he does the same. I live in Oklahoma, so it is a pleasant change of scenery."

Tom smiled. "We have known each other since we were teenagers. I think last time Jason was here, you couldn't come out for drinks with us and Joss."

"Right. Well, it's a pleasure to meet you."

There was a lull, and an awkward smile was all we could muster.

Tom continued. "The ladies at church were in a frenzy earlier. I heard there was a bit of a scuffle. How are you doing really, Thibault? You are the one who found her, aren't you? People say you had something to do with it. Did you?"

That startled me. Even sweet Tom thought I might have done it?

"You think..."

He interrupted me. "Sorry, I shouldn't have said so. You finding her body does not make you the murderer. We will see what the police have to say, and they haven't arrested you, so not guilty until proven otherwise. Am I right?" He chuckled.

I politely smiled. So that information hadn't circulated yet. And people believed I might have done it. Talking to him had taken my mind off things and made me relax, but it was rapidly fading.

Reagan hip-checked me. "Hey, pretty boss. Isn't it time for you to go have lunch with Sam? I am pretty sure I saw him waving at us not two minutes ago. Go ahead. I'll woman the booth."

Smiling at her in relief, I said goodbye to Tom and Jason, grabbed the sandwiches I had made this morning, and then almost ran to the Miracle Brew's booth.

"Hey Sam, ready for some grub? Wanna stay here or go on a stroll?" I noticed he had two of his people with him, and it didn't look like they were too busy yet. Or on second thought, they weren't busy anymore since they'd sold most of their goodies.

He removed his apron and shouted over his shoulder, "I'll be back soon," to his guys. We left, each starting on our sandwich in silence. After a couple minutes, he spoke. "So, how is it going on your side?"

"You know, same old, same old. Kids love petting the animals. Mamas look at the books as if they were diamonds, then only pick some for the kiddos. Older folks enjoy the chat probably more than the books. Irate church ladies accuse you of being a murderer. Business as usual."

He snorted. "Well, if it's any consolation, all the retellings I got of that particular encounter were in your favor. They all say she was out of line, and most are commending you for not answering. Others are a bit puzzled why you didn't fight back. I pointed out no matter what you said, you were condemned in her eyes. They all seemed to agree, kind of. But consensus is you're a friendly guy who couldn't ever have done such a heinous thing. Jack's confirmation you didn't do it is spreading."

"Yeah, nice to hear, I guess. I don't know how I feel about this, on top of everything else. There was so much pain in her eyes. I don't know. After two years, it saddens me that someone could look at me and think 'murderer.' Yes, yes, I know, it's just one person. And serial killers usually look like great, upstanding citizens, so you never know who is guilty, but it hurts all the same."

"I know. Come on, let's go back to my tent. I saved you an orange-and-chocolate scone. Thought you might need it." In his tent, I devoured the treat as if I would never touch another one in my life.

When I went back to my booth after saying goodbye to

Sam and his guys, I noticed it was almost two. Perfect. I could start packing up with Reagan and go back to the farm. We only stayed in the mornings because the afternoon crowd was less interested in books. They came for the music and antiquities.

That part was fun but not while manning a booth. Under different circumstances, I would come back around 4:00 p.m. with Sam to roam. See what we could exchange. Maybe enjoy a beer or two, listen to the bands on stage. But after everything, I wanted to relax at home.

Reagan offered to put the books back in the library if I could give her a lift. After dropping her off, I went home, done with the week and ready to relax for a few hours before having to face the library the next day.

# 16

---

**The Week Following The Murder – Monday**

*M*onday already. Last week felt so long. I hadn't been ready for a new one when I woke up. I went for a quick run and a cardio workout in hopes that it would put me in the right frame of mind to tackle the day. The whole week, even.

Seeing Thibault at the market yesterday was both good and bad. I couldn't get past the uncertainty and hurt in his eyes. That he'd talked to me at all was great. Despite my less-than-stellar moves this past week—hell, these past two years—he was still willing to listen, at least. And I meant what I'd said. I'd known deep down, probably from the beginning, he didn't do it. And I would have happily kissed him all night if my brain and my mother hadn't interrupted.

I arrived at the station as John was leaving. "Hey, Johnny, are you on a call right now?"

"No. I am going on patrol with Matthew, our new guy. Anything I can help you with?"

"Would you mind stopping on the boulevard at Hampton Street and check with the businesses if they have any cameras? We only spotted one on Hampton Street but others might be hidden. I left the list with George."

"Sure thing, Jack. I'll keep you posted."

"Thank you."

I went to my desk and found Marcus and coffee waiting for me.

"Hey, Jack."

"Hey. You are in early. Everything all right? I just saw John. He will canvass the shops for cameras."

"Great, J. I am fine. Just itching to get started, I guess."

I felt the same, though I wouldn't have minded an extra day off.

"What do we have today?" I asked.

"Mostly print and interviews. I checked on Sally Anne's phone. It is still not unlocked."

"Do we know who is coming in first?"

"I think the library guys, but let's ask George and see."

Our first interview of the day was with Charlene, George informed us. We moved to the conference room and waited for her there while we each reviewed our notes.

"So, are y'all going to stop that woman from spreading nonsense or should I?" Charlene came into the room.

"Hey, Charlene, what are you talking about?"

"Don't play with me, boys. Dorothy has been spreading rumors about my Thibault all of yesterday. It's barely nine thirty, and we have already had three people ask if it was true."

Poppy seeds. Exactly what we needed. I was surprised the chief hadn't asked to see us to know what was taking so long. Though by normal standards four days wasn't long, with Dorothy making a ruckus, I had a feeling the mayor would be breathing down our boss's neck in no time.

"Sorry, Charlene," I replied. "We told her Thibault was innocent yesterday at the market, but unfortunately we cannot do anything else. Unless she threatens him or us, our hands are tied." And even then, we couldn't do much.

We went over her statement and took her prints, and she left. Not satisfied but a little calmer, at least.

Next was Gwendolyn, Thibault's colleague who had closed the library on Thursday night.

"So, Detectives, what is this about? Are we all being investigated? Do you need my statement as well? What is this nonsense I hear about Thibault being the primary suspect? You don't believe he did it, do you? That is the biggest load of baloney I have ever heard, and I hope our police department has people intelligent enough to realize what a colossal mistake it would be to think that. He can't even kill spiders." She looked so prim and proper at all times, never raising her voice, sweet as rice pudding. I forgot she could be a spitfire when people she cared about were threatened.

I was quick to reassure her the prints were to eliminate them as suspects, as we were bound to have found some of their prints on surfaces like the door or desk. I explained evidence had surfaced showing Thibault had done nothing, and yes, we were working on other leads. I inquired about Thursday night, the doorstopper, and locking the door on her way out.

For a moment, she looked taken aback, and I wondered why. Blushing and looking sheepish, she blurted, "I always forget the doorstopper. Oh my gosh, don't tell me someone took it again? I swear I try to remember to bring it back in, but I can't remember if I did on Thursday. I was a little distracted. My phone pinged with a text from my husband, and I was replying as I went out, so it is possible I left it outside. The door—no, I definitely locked it. You might see it on the video. Did you get the tape?"

I assured her we had, took her prints, and ushered her out.

Nathaniel came and went quietly as well. He told me he hadn't known Sally Anne very well and she had always steered clear of him, as she was, "One of those folks who believe everything they hear on the TV and was afraid I would probably hold her at gunpoint for those books she took after hours or something. Not that she ever knew we all knew. She was thick as a doorknob and thought herself sneaky and clever." Even though Thibault was one of the few she'd had loud arguments with, Sally Anne was probably not as popular as she'd believed she was. It became even clearer as the day went on.

Reagan was quick, as she was here on her lunch break and needed to hurry back to school. Her scowl was mighty. As she left, Marcus remarked, "Wait till she grows up some more, and you two can have contests. I just hope she doesn't become a law enforcement officer. One of you scowling is enough to scare the suspects and innocents alike."

He jumped when Reagan rasped from the door, "Thanks for the compliment. I want to become a lawyer and district attorney if I can. Between me and him, we should be able to put people behind bars and keep them there." She high-fived me, grabbed the sandwich bag she had forgotten on the table, and left again.

As we went, we added their prints to the system to exclude them and only looked through the database for ones we needed.

After a quick break for lunch, we braced ourselves for the ladies from the HPS to come in.

They all started the same—"That man did it! Why is he not arrested?"—and quickly dissolved into telling us who else it could be when they saw our skeptical faces and we repeated what we'd said at the market. They had all gotten along all right with Sally Anne. But after we pushed them a little, each one had some not-so-pleasant things to report about the deceased.

"Well, she was the treasurer, you know, but she was a real penny pincher. It was difficult to get her to agree to anything. She used to pitch quite the hissy fit if we disagreed."

"She didn't like homosexuals, for sure. I respect everyone's opinion, and at first, I understood her and what she meant. After all, rumor has it her husband did not leave her for a young woman but a younger man. Things changed for me when my niece came out. I understand scripture, but she is such a wonderful girl. I don't think she chose to go against the will of God.

"But Sally Anne kept telling me and the rest of us how it wasn't normal. I shouldn't let my sister raise a child in sin, and great groups could help my niece. I just needed to bring her over to church. I told her off, but she kept coming back to it."

"She always looked down her nose at people. To be honest, I won't say I was happy to see her husband leave her for a younger person—and rumor has it, a man at that—but I wasn't sorry about it either. It took her down a peg or two. Oh, she rallied fast, preaching worse than ever. Last I heard, she might have found someone. But she kept mum on it. She only hinted at it, hoping we would ask questions."

Sally Anne's coworkers didn't have much to add.

Once we were done, the chief asked to see us in his office. Dorothy had indeed gone to the mayor, who wanted answers, and therefore so did the chief. "So, gentlemen, any progress? The mayor told me we have a suspect, but he is not in custody?"

Marcus was first to answer. "We made some progress, but

we are still going through interviews. The suspect you are talking about, I guess, is Thibault Abrams. Mary showed us evidence it couldn't be him, Chief."

"Really? Then why do the mayor and a woman named Dorothy keep insisting we arrest him?"

"He is gay, sir, and often argued with the victim and Dorothy. They have been after him since he arrived in town. The video we have of the library shows two men entering it, and based on Mary's comparison, Thibault doesn't match their height. In addition, based on the coroner's report, the man who killed Sally Anne was taller than her, which Thibault isn't," I added.

"I see. So, do we have any actual suspects?"

"Not so far, sir. We need you to sign off on warrant requests. John and the new guy, Matthew, canvassed the streets this morning. They were able to spot more cameras than we did, belonging to bank ATMs, and they are requesting warrants. We need one for Sally Anne's network provider as well. Her phone should unlock anytime now, but if she deleted calls or texts, we won't be able to see them. So we figured going with her provider should help."

"All right, send me your warrant requests, and I will pass them to the judge now. Is this Dorothy woman going to be in today?"

"Yes, sir."

"Tell George to let me know when she comes in. I want to be present, just in case."

"Will do, sir, thank you."

We left his office. As there was still no sign of Dorothy, we worked on our warrants.

When she finally came in, George ushered her to the conference room. She eyed us suspiciously, then sneered. "You are not arresting that deviant demon, but you are arresting me?" she exclaimed. No screeching so far. We were doing better than yesterday at least.

"We are not here to make arrests. We are only taking prints from everyone who had access to the library to eliminate them from the investigation. Could you please tell us where the meetings for the HPS usually took place?" Marcus replied.

She looked at both of us. "We were using one or two of the tables in the main room. Better light and more space than in the employee lounge."

"When we were at Sally Anne's, we noticed a bowl and dog food. Did her dog pass away recently?"

"No, why?"

"Do you know where the dog might be, then? It wasn't there, and her niece hasn't arrived in town yet."

"What?" she screeched. "What do you mean it wasn't there? What did you do with Misty?"

"I am sorry, Dorothy, but there was no dog at the duck pond and when we didn't see"—I paused, looked at my notes, and added—"Misty at Sally Anne's home, we assumed the dog had died or was with one of Sally Anne's friends already."

"It isn't, you incompetent men. That murderer Thibault must have stolen it. Poor little Misty."

"Dorothy, as we told you already, Thibault had nothing to do with the murder. I understand in your grief you need someone to blame, but casting suspicion on an innocent could cause more damage. Now, did you know of anyone who might have a grudge against her?"

"What? No, Sally Anne was a good person. She didn't have problems with anyone."

She started crying then, and any questions we tried to ask were left unanswered. After taking her prints, we let her go.

We accompanied her to the reception desk, and she was able to give George a description of the little dog as well as a picture of Sally Anne with Misty, to be sent to everyone in the precinct, vets, and animal associations around town and the county.

On Tuesday Sally Anne's phone finally unlocked, but as with her computer, nothing stood out.

I hoped the warrants would bring us answers.

## Thibault

The week so far had been uneventful. Monday had been tough on me. Even though I wasn't the one opening on Mondays, I went in at 7:00 a.m. I walked in and stayed in the staff room for a few minutes, switched on all the lights, and made my way slowly toward the front desk. Once there, I felt paralyzed. Cold sweat trickled down my back. A text on my phone from my sister startled me and pushed me forward.

I opened all the shutters and windows to clear the air out of the room. I could still smell the flowery and coppery smells from Friday, even if I knew there was little chance of their lingering. What was truly in the air was the scent of chemicals used by the cleaning crew. I tried sitting at the front desk but quickly abandoned the idea. I could only see Sally Anne's body.

When Charlene came in, she found me in the stacks putting away the books from the market. That gave us both a fright, as she didn't expect me there and I hadn't heard her come in.

From there, things went all right, especially after I settled at a small desk right next to our front desk. It made me available for people but didn't force me to sit where Sally Anne had been.

People were good. Most asked questions on the murder and if we had any information on how the investigation was going. We all had to repeat that no, we didn't know anything, least of all me, and they should ask the police or check the newspaper. Dorothy came in screeching at me that she had told the mayor everything. Charlene was quick to stop her and tell her to leave. And the look on people's faces as she was leaving told her what they thought, which wasn't that I was guilty. Their trust was a relief to me, but the gleam in her eyes told me this wasn't over.

On Tuesday, people delighted in telling me the police had given a small statement stating proof showed I had nothing to do with it. Some gleefully said as much in front of Dorothy, looking at her with raised eyebrows. If she could have slammed the door on her way out, she would have happily done so.

Things came to a head on Wednesday late afternoon. Around 6:00 p.m., I was almost ready to close when her voice assaulted me once again, yelling at me and calling me a murderer. I had had enough of her and her accusations, so I clapped back.

"Oh, quit it, you old harpy. You know damn well I had nothing to do with it. So climb off your high horse and stop with that nonsense. Nobody believes you, and from what I heard, even the detectives told you off!"

"It's all my fault she is dead," she whispered, dropping on a nearby chair.

Well, butter my butt and call me a biscuit, like they said around here. I certainly hadn't expected that. "What do you mean?" I asked.

"I am the one who told her about the stupid dating app. She met someone on it, but lately it looked like it took a turn." She started crying. I crouched down in front of her and passed her a couple of tissues, patting her hand awkwardly.

"That wasn't your fault. We all meet creeps on these sites. What happened?"

"She met a man. At first they hit it off, but the messages became a little menacing." She paused and cleared her throat. "She talked about you and others like you. The person on the other side didn't appreciate it and didn't seem to share our views. So Sally Anne tried to break it off. But the man kept messaging her. She blocked him and deleted their conversation, but new messages appeared with different usernames. She never showed them to me. That night before she went for a walk with Misty, we were on the phone, and she received another one of those horrible messages."

"It might mean nothing. Did you tell the detectives about this?"

Blushing, she shook her head. In a small voice, she said, "I know I should, but what will the town think of me, knowing I am using an app to find myself a man? And I don't want to sully Sally Anne's reputation. I hoped they would find it themselves, but she must have left the hidden mode on."

"Hidden mode?"

"Yes, it's very nifty. You can have it as a setting or something on your phone so anyone looking at your screen or scrolling through your apps won't know what it is. They would only notice if you got a message from the app. And even then, it's still kind of disguised." She pulled out her phone to show me the app. I made a note of the name "Whynotme" and decided to look it up later.

"Do you know her username?"

"Yes, PrettySallySC."

I couldn't say it surprised me.

Trying to reassure her, I patted her hand some more. I told

her I would try and figure out if the detectives or someone at the precinct had noticed the app, and if not, I would let them know. She left shortly after that, still sniffing. The poor woman. I wasn't sure she had any close friends beyond Sally Anne. In her shoes, I am not sure what I would have done.

**The Week Following The Murder - Wednesday**

Shortly after talking with Dorothy, I went home and downloaded the app. I looked up "PrettySallySC," and as her profile was still active, I added her as a contact.

Remembering Jack had given me his number, I sent him a text to let him know I had discovered something which might help with his investigation.

When I checked my postbox, I found another letter waiting for me. I put it on my kitchen table and brought the other one over as well, then set out to prepare some food. I would read them while I ate.

I was ready for supper when there was a knock at my door. I tensed. This was highly unusual, and with everything going on lately, it scared me.

When I went to the door, I was surprised to find Jack. "What are you doing here?"

"Can I come in?"

Remembering my manners, reluctantly, I let him in.

Before dinner burned, I rushed back to the kitchen to switch off the stove. I turned around to find Jack had followed me. "What do you want, Jack?"

"You wanted to tell me something. So here I am."

"I meant tomorrow at the precinct. I thought you would text me back to let me know when you and Marcus were available so I could pop over. I did not expect you to just show up at my house."

"I wanted to see you, and I thought you meant you wanted to talk about what happened." He saw the letters then. "What are these? Are you seeing someone?"

"What are you talking about?"

"These look like the other love letters you have, don't they?"

"Are you really doing this right now? Are you jealous? And what do you mean, 'like the other ones?'" I griped.

"I mean the ones in your closet. And no, I am not jealous, but if you are with someone, why the hell did you kiss me?"

As he talked, he started stalking toward me, cornering me where I was standing in front of the table. I turned us around, pushing him against it. "I am not seeing anyone, not that it would be any of your business if I was."

"It is my business if you kiss me while seeing someone else."

"For the record, Jack, you kissed me. I simply kissed you back. I don't appreciate you acting as if you know me or like you have a right to tell me what to do. For your information, if I am with someone, I am all in. I don't toy with them, I don't breathe hot and cold, like you have been doing, and I don't go around kissing other people."

His gaze fixed on my lips. He wasn't paying attention to what I was saying anymore, growing hard against me. I leaned over him while talking, and he was half bent backward on the table.

I couldn't help it. I leaned in and bit his lip. The moan coming out of his mouth was like music to my ears. I let my lips explore his cheek, ear, neck. Nibbling, licking, biting. The symphony of sounds leaving his lips ramped up my own desire.

He moved his hands, placing one on my back and the other on my arse. I let him for a second, enjoying the full body contact, then grabbed them and placed them on the table over his head.

"Leave them right here," I rasped. He nodded.

My own hands wandered, first over his hips. Then, finger-nails raking along the skin of his torso, I dragged his shirt off and over his head. When he didn't place his hands back on the table, I growled and bit his collarbone gently. He complied with a moan, knowing instinctively what I wanted. I leaned back a little and took in the expanse of his skin, the tattoos along his arms disappearing behind his shoulders. Tattoos I didn't know existed but added another layer of complexity to this beautiful man.

Moving back down, I took my time, exploring his neck with tongue and teeth and slowly making my way to his nipples. Not everyone was sensitive there, but his hips lifted again to meet mine as soon as I nipped at his left nipple, telling me he wasn't one of those people.

I played with both, laving them with my tongue before blowing air on them. His eyes had glazed over, and the emerald was almost gone, his pupils blown by arousal. Still gazing at him, I mouthed the tattoos decorating his torso. Going ever lower, my hands busily unbuttoned his jeans, eager to get at what was underneath.

What I felt made me pause, and I briefly glimpsed fear

before his gaze turned defiant. Hmmm. I took my eyes off his to see what exactly he was wearing. The sexiest pair of boxer shorts cradled his balls and cock in the most gorgeous way. Gently, I traced his shaft through the lacy blue fabric, the prettiest mix of delicate and enticing.

Leaning back, I gently mouthed him over the fabric. I watched him through my lashes as he released the breath he was holding in the sweetest sigh. I nibbled at the skin above his waistband and, using my teeth, slowly lowered the fabric. His head fell back to the table with a soft thud.

I wanted to take him in my mouth but didn't have a condom on me. I'd never had a need for them in my kitchen before. I gently licked and nibbled at him and couldn't resist kissing the head of his cock. My hands were busy lowering my pants, glad I usually wore loose-fitting pairs when alone at home. Needing skin-on-skin contact for what I had in mind next, I made quick work of them and my shirt.

Lifting one of his legs, I divested it of his shoe and pants and quickly did the same with the other. I went back up his body, kissing and nipping him all over. I pulled him toward me, his arse barely hanging off the table, wrapping his legs around the back of mine.

Enjoying the feel of his beard on my skin, I pressed gentle kisses to his throat while grasping both of our cocks in my hand. He was slender but long, fitting perfectly against my own thick cock. Applying pressure, I slowly moved along our shafts. He lifted his head off the table, capturing my lips in a searing kiss, swallowing our moans and gasps.

I moved my hand faster, using our combined precum as lubricant. One of his hands grabbed my free one. Our lips separated, mine going to his neck as his body arched off the table. His breathing changed, and I looked into his eyes.

Undulating my hips, I pumped my hand faster, our cocks gliding and grinding against each other.

He tensed. His uttered "Thibault" was my only warning before his release hit. His full-body shiver almost dislodged me while his hand clasped mine to the point of hurting. Watching his face as hot ribbons of cum plastered his chest, I kept rubbing our cocks together. I released him as soon as he finished, knowing how sensitive it could get. Pumping myself faster over him, I painted his chest and cock with my release a few seconds later, whispering his name while looking in his eyes.

I collapsed on top of him. Our breathing slowed down while the cum between us cooled. He tensed beneath me, bringing me back to reality. This could go two ways. Completely awkward, with Jack retreating in himself and hiding away from me. Or I could take control this time and make sure we could handle this. If not as friends, then at least like the two adults we were.

I lifted my head up and gently kissed his lips.

"Now." He opened his mouth, and I placed a finger on it. "Nope. You're not going to talk or run off. Not this time. I am going to move and get us a washcloth. Then we can talk about it over dinner, or we can table it for now and talk about what I called you over for. This doesn't need to be awkward if we don't let it."

Frowning, he mulled it over for a second, then nodded with a tentative smile. "Sounds fair to me."

His stomach growling made me smile in return, while he groaned, covering his face with his arm.

Laughing, I stood back up. I went to my half bath right off the kitchen. I took a washcloth and cleaned myself up, then went back to the kitchen to look after Jack. He was still sitting on my kitchen table looking beautiful, soft cock and golden skin on display. When he moved, the muscles rippled under his skin, making his tattoos dance.

I stood, about to clean him, when he tried to grab the cloth from my hand, looking down.

I lifted his chin with my left hand, holding onto the washcloth. "Please, let me do this for you?"

He nodded, and I gently wiped him clean. I traced the tattoo of a hummingbird on his left bicep. "Your tattoos are beautiful. I didn't know you had ink."

"Thank you," he whispered. "I got most of them in Columbia and Charleston. We don't have a tattoo artist yet in Weatherboro. Every time a new shop opens, I keep all my fingers crossed for a tattoo parlor but no luck so far. The last one I got was a little under two years ago." He pointed at one the size of a small fist, with a calligraphy R surrounded by distinct animal prints.

"That is very sweet." Smiling at him, I moved back. I rinsed the cloth and dropped it into my laundry room.

I came back to the kitchen to the sound of Jack's stomach growling. He had put his clothes back on, and I grabbed my shirt off his hands and put it on a kitchen chair.

I moved to the cupboards and put out plates. Good thing I always made too much food so I could either freeze it or keep it for the next day.

I served us and was about to move to the kitchen table when I caught Jack's eye. His blush was beautiful. I shook my head. "Grab your plate. We will eat in the dining room. That table hasn't seen any action in a while, and I think this one has seen enough for one night, don't you?"

His rich laugh followed me to the dining room.

Once I placed my plate and cutlery, I walked back to the kitchen for drinks and came back with them and the letters.

We dug in silently.

"All right, Jack. Do you have your phone or a notepad handy?" I asked, finally looking at him over my ratatouille and breaded chicken.

"Yes, just give me one second. My phone would be best. This is too good to grow cold."

"Charmer."

He winked. Once he set his phone on the table and started recording, I explained what had happened at the library.

"I knew she was hiding something. What's Sally Anne's username?"

"PrettySallySC. Apparently, Sally Anne had one serious suitor. Things turned sour when she expressed her views on homosexuality. She blocked the person. Soon after that, she started receiving threats from different accounts."

"What?" Jack half shouted. "What do you mean 'threats'?"

"I don't know anything else. The other thing is apparently this app has what Dorothy called a stealth mode. So you wouldn't see it on Sally Anne's phone unless she received a notification." I pulled out my phone and showed Jack how to find the hidden mode. He sent a message from my profile to Sally Anne's.

We finished our dinner in silence.

"I need to grab something upstairs. Give me a second, and I'll show you what I meant earlier."

I rushed upstairs and grabbed the box of letters in my closet. The top one had been moved, so I placed it back where it belonged.

Once again seated next to Jack at the dining table, I took a deep breath. "I started receiving these letters a year and a half ago. I don't know who they are from. At first they arrived once a month, always on a Thursday night, and I would find them on Friday mornings. In the past two or three months, it became once a week. Until last Thursday." Jack raised his brows at that.

I pulled out the letters and let Jack read them. They all started and ended the same: "Dear Thibault," and signed "Always yours, your secret admirer." The content varied. Sometimes they were sweet, especially at the beginning, complimenting me about my looks or something I did. Some were aggressive or ranting.

Jack's eyebrows kept rising as he read. He looked at me, his face stuck in a frown. "Why didn't you report these? Do you have any idea who it could be?"

"I don't have a clue who it could be or I would have come to the police with them. The only person I can think of is this guy who ghosted me, as it happened a couple of weeks before these started."

"So why tell me now?"

I picked up the two still folded and unread letters. "This came after Sally Anne's murder, and I have a bad feeling. That's why I haven't read them yet. A changing pattern is never a good thing."

"Can I?"

I handed them over to Jack, holding my breath. Jack started the recording again. "This is Jack Tomlins. Reading letters sent by an anonymous person to Thibault Abrams. He received the first letter the day after the murder of Sally Anne Johnston."

He opened the first letter and let out a "Poppy seeds," followed by a "Fuck." Hearing him swear scared me more than the letters. He dropped the letter and opened the second one.

I pulled the letter he had dropped toward me and read.

*Dear Thibault,*

*I hope this finds you well, as always. I hope you found my little present to your liking. I hadn't planned this, but I thought you might be happy to see your long-time enemy gone. She went too far this time, and it was time someone took action.*

*Hope you can sleep better now, knowing that one less hater is alive.*

*I thought of leaving her in your home, but didn't want to disturb your peaceful sleep last night. And I know how much you love crime stories, so having her waiting for you in the temple of crime books seemed fitting.*

*Always yours,*

*Your secret admirer.*

I rushed to the bathroom to throw up.

A soft hand rubbed my back. Before turning around, I stood up, flushed the mess, and rinsed my mouth. Jack pulled me into his arms, enfolding me and holding me tight. I shuddered.

"What does the other one say?"

"I am not sure you should know."

"Please?"

"In that one, they are ranting over Dorothy." He paused. "And me. Whoever they are, they know we went home together on Friday night and kissed. Did you tell anyone?"

"Only Sam and George. We were at the Tavern before you arrived. I didn't notice anyone, but you didn't see us and we heard every word you said to Marcus, so if someone was in the booth behind you or the one behind me, then they could have heard my version or yours."

"All right, so no way of knowing."

"No." I took a step back. "This is my fault, isn't it?"

"No. No. Don't think so. The actions of someone else are not your responsibility."

"Sally Anne is dead because of me."

"No, Sally Anne is dead because someone decided to take it upon themselves to be judge, jury, and executioner over her fights with you. Now we need to make sure whoever did this does not hurt you or anyone else. These letters might help. I will need the name of the app you used a year and a half ago and your username. We will get a warrant and request the records from the app company. It will be okay."

I sagged against Jack, the weight of everything bringing me down.

"Come on, sweetheart. Let's get you to bed."

"It's not even eight in the evening."

"All right, do you want to sit and read or watch something?"

I nodded. Jack chuckled against my hair and steered me toward the sitting room, setting me on the sofa and switching on the TV. After settling on a *Jurassic Park* rerun, he left, pottering around my dining room and the kitchen. I lay down on the couch, the letter and Sally Anne's body on the counter blurring in my mind.

Jack came back in, pulled my knitted cover over me, lifted my head, sat on the couch, and placed my head back gently on his thighs.

I must have fallen asleep, as the next thing I knew he was placing me gently in my bed. Jack made to leave, and I grabbed his hand before he could go anywhere.

"Stay with me?"

He didn't say anything, just kissed me gently. I burrowed under my covers, and when I heard him go down the stairs, I let the tears fall.

I gasped when the left side of the bed dipped. Jack's citrus smell hit me before his soft voice. "It's just me. Try to sleep, baby."

"Thank you," I whispered back. I rolled toward him. Feeling his sturdy arms surround me, I fell into a troubled sleep.

## 18

---

JACK

**The Week Following The Murder - Thursday**

Coming to awareness surrounded by Thibault's scent felt right. Lavender and pine invaded my senses as he moved against me. We were both lying on our sides, my arms wrapped tight around him. I had never really woken up next to someone before. The events of the previous night came back to me, making me tense. Then I remembered what Thibault had said. This didn't have to be awkward. Did we need to talk about it? Most likely, but for right now, I tightened my arms around him, pulling him closer.

I nuzzled his neck and hair gently, inhaling his scent. Something moved up my legs, and a light weight settled on them. One of the cats sat on me. The others were scattered around the bed.

The sounds of Lady Gaga and Rihanna mixed, waking Thibault up. He turned around in my arms, pecked me on the lips, and whispered, "Good morning, Detective."

"Morning," I whispered back. He rolled away from me, taking his cell phone in hand and switching the alarm off. I rolled to my side of the bed and did the same.

"I am going to take a shower. Do you want to join me for breakfast before going to work?" he asked from behind me.

"I think I need to go home. I didn't set my alarm for early enough, and I have to change clothes."

I looked at him. A little disappointed, he shrugged but smiled at me.

"No problem." He was about to leave the room when he turned around. He stalked toward me, stood on his toes, and gave me another sweet kiss. "Have a good day, then."

In half a daze, I walked out, remembering at the last second to take the letters I had put back in the box last night.

What happened last night between us was both wonderful and scary. And, once again, so domestic. I would love to have more of those mornings with Thibault.

We needed to talk about things before we fell into something that we both wanted but were too scared to talk about.

But first, I needed to concentrate on work. After a quick shower, a change of clothes, and coffee, I went to the station. I arrived at the same time as Marcus. I placed the letters on my desk and stared at them.

Marcus cleared his throat and asked, "Jack, what's going on? You have been staring at these for the past ten minutes with a frown and a smile on your face."

I looked at him. "Sorry. What?"

He laughed. "What's up with you today?"

I shook my head, trying to clear it. This wasn't like me at all. For both Sally Anne and Thibault, I needed to get my head back in the game. "Grab Sally Anne's phone and meet me in the conference room. I have something to tell you and show you."

He looked puzzled but nodded. "Sure, give me two minutes."

I made my way to the conference room and waited for him there. Pulling out my phone, I let him listen to what Thibault had said of his conversation with Dorothy. He switched on Sally Anne's device, and there was Thibault's notification.

We looked into the app and checked every conversation, but there were no messages with one person in particular. Just some small talk here and there. We noticed several blocked users.

Marcus shook his head. "It could be any of them. I have been solicited by creeps and weirdos often enough on both Grindr and Tinder to know she might have received requests and blocked them as well as whoever this person might be."

"We need to put another warrant through, then. They should be able to retrieve and send us all the conversations she has under her username. Hopefully, they keep that data."

"Ok. Now what's in the box?"

I told him about Thibault's stalker, replaying the part of the conversation I had on my phone as well.

Reading these, he looked disgusted. "I understand his reasoning on not wanting to open a case for this, but he could have told me."

"When?" I asked. I knew they were friendly, but I hadn't realized they were close.

"We try to have drinks once a month. Most of the time with Sam or George or Tabitha if they can join. A few times on our own."

"You two hang out?"

Smiling, Marcus looked at me. "Don't worry. We had one date two years ago. Trust me, he is not my type. I never really talked to you about him because there was nothing to say. You seemed to have something against him, so I thought it was better to keep him out of our conversations. If I had known about certain feelings you have for the guy, I might have talked. It might have pushed you into making a move earlier."

"Oh, shut up. I am not easily manipulated."

Marcus laughed. "No, but it would have been fun to see you squirm. So what else happened last night? How did you end up at Thibault's?"

"He sent me a text asking when we could talk about the case, and I thought I might go and see what he had to say. That's it."

"It was so easy?"

"Yes. Get that smirk off your face, and let's get to work, see if we can contact the people from the app. I want to check with Mary about those videos from the ATMs."

"Spoilsport. Something happened, I can tell. I guess I will learn about it in a year or so..." Marcus trailed off. "Or I could ask Thibault. He is less tight-lipped than you are."

My growl made him laugh harder. I stalked out of the room and got to business.

**The Week Following The Murder – Saturday**

Frustration was ramping up. We had clues but nothing else. No suspect, really. Mary found a car going through the streets leading to the library around five that Friday morning, but she could only get a partial plate number. That combined with what she thought might be the make and model had gone into our systems, but nothing came through.

Around the same time, Joss, the one who found all the blood, had been jogging toward the duck pond. We called him in, and he confirmed seeing the car. He had given a description of it, but apart from some stickers, he didn't have much more to add to his previous statement.

I was sitting at my desk ready to pull my hair out while Marcus read everything we had once again. Then we heard barking coming from the front desk. Curious, we went to check it out.

"Hey, guys," George greeted us. "Look what I found while I was walking this morning."

We looked at each other, then back at George.

"Hey, George, who is this little guy?"

"I am not sure. He seemed to have escaped his masters this morning. The leash was still attached, and he was tangled up in a bush when I found him. There is a number on the tag. I was about to call but realized I would be late for work."

He pulled his phone out and tried to key in the number, but the dog kept wriggling. He handed me the device. "Jack, can you put the number in? I'll call it out to you, but I can't hold him and type at the same time."

After he called the number out to me, I dialed it. The phone kept ringing. Mary came out of her room holding a phone.

"Hey, Mary, we didn't know you had a dog. What's his name?"

"I don't have a dog. What are you talking about? I was in the evidence room checking what else needed to be processed in the murder case, and Sally Anne's phone started ringing off the hook. Thought you might want to pick up or call back."

Marcus and I both froze, then turned back to George, who was looking at the dog with horror and surprise written on his face.

"Mary, could you please take the dog and get him

processed? Call a vet if you need help. Tell the chief we might need him in the interrogation room," I said.

Marcus looked at me, startled. George's look was one of shock, sadness, and hurt.

"George, give Mary the dog and let's go. I think we need to have a chat. Marcus, grab the evidence box from Thursday, please."

I let George precede me and followed him to the interview room.

Once we were both seated, I pulled out my notepad. "So, George, could you please tell me in detail when and where you found Sally Anne's dog?"

"I just told you, Jack." His tone wasn't so much aggressive as hurt.

"Please, humor me."

"I was walking to the precinct this morning. I live at the junction between De Treville Road and Thompson Street. I enjoy walking to work on warm days like today. I walked up Thompson Street, then crossed onto Sanders Street and walked up St. Lucas. I came across the dog at the beginning of St Lucas. He was caught in a bush, and I heard him yip and bark. I was able to untangle him and walked him here."

"Did you see anyone on the streets or try to call out to see if someone was missing him before walking with him to the precinct?"

"There was no one. I looked up and down the street and called out, but nobody answered. There was no name or address on the collar, but he looked well cared for. I was surprised no one was calling out for him."

Marcus came in a second later with the box. Before the door closed, I saw the chief entering the little room behind the one-way mirror.

"Thanks, George. Did you know Sally Anne well?"

"What? No. Hell, I got the occasional lecture on my sins for being gay, but I always nodded, which wasn't what she was aiming for, so she used to leave me alone."

"Did you ever go on a date with Thibault Abrams?"

"What?"

Marcus looked as puzzled as George.

"Did you ever go on a date with Thibault when he first moved here or in the two years he has lived in Weatherboro?"

"I don't understand, Jack. What does this have to do with me finding Sally Anne's dog? What's next? Are you going to ask me where I was last Thursday night or if I killed her?" He glowered, getting angrier by the second.

"Please, answer the question."

"I went on a date with him, I think the first month he was here. We went somewhere to eat, can't remember where. We made out in the car. Laughed as there was absolutely no spark and decided to be friends. He was close to Sam already, and the three of us hung out together. Why?"

I ignored George's question and Marcus's questioning looks.

"Are you on any dating apps?"

"Not anymore. I used to be on Grindr but got tired of the creeps and older gentlemen looking for a 'twink to destroy.'"

"Could you please show me your phone?"

He looked at me, then at Marcus, and reluctantly pulled his phone out, unlocked it, and passed it to me.

I looked for Whynotme and Grindr but didn't find either. "I am going to need the email address you use to register to apps."

"What for, Jack? What is this about?"

"Write it down, please."

He did so, reluctantly.

"Do you own a typewriter?"

"Yes. You know I do. Why? Did I send anonymous letters declaring my undying love to Thibault and my hatred to Sally Anne?"

I opened the box, pulled out the letters, and fanned them out in front of him.

George blanched. "Jack, Marcus. Do I need a lawyer? What is this?"

"These are letters sent to Thibault for the past year and a half. They are all from a typewriter. I know you own several. Would you let us check yours against this font?"

He leaned back in his chair and crossed his arms. A knock at the door made him jump.

Marcus went to open the door. He gestured for me to follow him out.

"What the hell is going on, Jack?" Marcus barked at me once we were outside.

"He is friends with Thibault, owns a typewriter, and conveniently found Sally Anne's dog this morning. Don't you think it's a lot of coincidence?"

The chief cleared his throat, gesturing at Matthew and John.

"Hi, guys. Perfect. Could you please go to George's house and search it? Look for dog food?"

"No," John answered.

"What do you mean 'no'?"

"It wasn't George."

"How the hell would you know? I know he is our friend and colleague, but..."

John interrupted me. "But nothing. It's not George. I was with my patrol car, coming back this morning, when I saw a guy looking around frantically on Sanders Street. I stopped my car to see if I could help. When he noticed me, he took off before I could get out of the car. I had seen George at the crossing between St. Jefferies and Sanders Street, alone. He waved when he passed me at the light. I was about to drive off when I saw George on St. Lucas Street. I called out to him, but he didn't hear. He was bending down in the bushes and came out bedraggled, holding a dog in his arms. He looked at the tag but almost dropped his phone trying to dial, as the dog kept jumping and wriggling. He picked up the dog and came here."

I rubbed my forehead. Poppy seeds. I had jumped the gun again, hadn't I?

Matthew stepped forward. "And I know where George was the night of the murder. I came to town early, to settle down before starting here. I needed a drink that night, and I went to the Tavern, as people had recommended it. I saw George there. I arrived around seven thirty p.m. and left a little after ten. George was still there, chatting with a woman. Tall, brunette, beautiful. Wedding ring on her finger. I am pretty sure they were together the whole time."

God. An idiot. I was turning into a fool. First accusing Thibault of murder because of my attraction to him and now jumping on George because we were going nowhere on this and he had found Sally Anne's dog.

Nodding, I went back in, closely followed by Marcus, who left the door open.

I sat down. "George. I am sorry. Could you please tell me where and who you were with the night of the murder?"

"I was with Tabitha from six p.m. till eleven, I think. Are you finally going to tell me why you asked all of this? I am guessing something new came up since you are leaving the door open."

"I am really sorry. Thibault has been receiving anonymous

letters from a typewriter, which included threats against Sally Anne. You own one. And you coming in with Sally Anne's dog felt like too much to be just a coincidence."

"So you just assumed that I was guilty. Jesus. I told Thibault to cut you some slack, but maybe he shouldn't have and neither should I. If instead of jumping to conclusions, you would have asked questions, I could have told you one of my typewriters was stolen a year ago during the break-ins. I filed a report. And if you would have come to me when you got these"—George gestured at the letters—"I could have told you that the first ones were made by a font on a computer, not a typewriter. But they wrote the rest on a typewriter. Mine, most likely, as there is a little smudge under every A, which was a defect and one of the reasons I left it on display instead of using it. The others were all in my office that I keep locked."

"How can you see the difference?"

"I received my first typewriter as a gift from my grand-mother when I was ten. When I started working, I bought more. Most of them have their own little unique thing. I received letters a few years ago, but I couldn't figure out what type of machine they used. So I wrote back, and they told me about that font."

"When did you receive these letters? Was it similar to these?"

He looked startled at Marcus's question. "No. No. It was a fan letter." He must have seen the confusion on our faces, as he added, "That's all I am going to say. Can I go now, or do you need something else?"

"We will confirm with Tabitha for last Thursday. I am sorry, George. I don't know what else to say."

"Promise me when you find who killed Sally Anne and is scaring my friend, you make sure you do your job right. You can check the system for my statement on the theft of my typewriter and a few other items from last year."

He left the room then, and I let my head fall on the desk with a thunk.

"Well, nice one, Jack. Of all the people to go off on, you had to pick George?" Marcus asked.

"I didn't pick George. He came in with the dog of a woman who was murdered. Said dog hadn't been seen since the murder. What did you want me to think?"

Marcus's eyes rolled so far back I could see the whites. "You were supposed to pause for a second and ask your friend, nicely, what he was doing with the dog. Jesus, that's the second time in a week. Out of the two of us, you are the gruff, cool-headed guy. This week you have been running around accusing the wrong people of murder. You need to put your head back in the game and stop losing focus."

"Detectives." We both turned to look at the chief. "I hope you two are happy. George..."

"He didn't quit, did he? I am sorry, sir. I will apologize again."

"No, Detective Tomlins, he didn't quit. He left for the day and should be back on Monday, hopefully. Before he left, he received a call from the wildlife wardens. They stopped a man they suspect of poaching. I sent an officer to pick him up. From what I understand, the description of his car matches Mary's video. They will provide you with the plates so Mary can check against our partial. You think you can handle the interview?"

"Yes, sir," Marcus replied. He looked at me, then added, "I'll lead."

We waited by the reception desk. The ranger arrived first, and we went to the conference room to talk. "Hey. Nice to see you again, Detectives."

"Likewise. What brings you here? We were told you found someone who might be of interest to us?"

"Yes. The suspect is Jason Swanton. We found him this morning not far from the dead buck last week. He had a rifle and hunting knife. We are pretty sure he is the poacher we have been looking for and thought you might be interested in talking to him."

"Yes, fantastic. We will have our team check the license plate."

John knocked on the door and came in. "Hey Jack, I took pictures of his car and sent them to Mary. He is waiting for you in the interrogation room. I left Matthew with him. He is already asking for a lawyer."

"Thanks, John."

We showed the warden where to stay so he could look into the interrogation room, and we went in. "Hi, Jason. I am Detective Marcus Elmer, and this is Senior Detective Jack Tomlins. You are here today on suspicion of poaching and murder."

"Murder?" Jason exclaimed, his eyes wide. "What are you talking about?"

While Marcus explained, I stepped outside and asked John, "Did you give Mary the rifle and knife? Could you please ask her to check the small piece of material we found at the duck pond against the knife?"

"Sure thing, Jack. Will do right away."

I went back in to find Jason shaking his head vehemently. "Whatever you think I did, I didn't. I don't know anyone named Sally Anne, and I have no clue who that Thibault guy is. I was only here for the poaching. I want a lawyer now. I am not saying anything else without one."

We walked back out. "This is not going anywhere, is it?" Marcus's shoulders slumped.

"He's definitely not telling us something. We need to think.

Let's go grab a coffee while we wait for his lawyer and see how we can approach this."

We went to the Miracle Brew. At the register, a voice called out to us. Sam and Thibault were sitting at a small coffee table in the corner, so we made our way there. I wasn't sure what was going to happen next, but I didn't want the entire coffee shop to hear.

"What is this we heard about you arresting George? What the hell?" Thibault whisper-shouted.

"We didn't arrest him. There was a bit of a misunderstanding."

"A misunderstanding is when you invite someone to a restaurant and you both show up at different times. It's not arresting someone on suspicion of murder," Sam growled.

"I screwed up. He came in with Sally Anne's dog, and he owns several typewriters. I jumped to conclusions."

"Hey, guys." We all turned at the sound of Tom's voice and waved at him.

Thibault asked, "So, twice in a week you jumped to conclusions, Detective? I always thought you were levelheaded, but I am starting to wonder what hides under that cool exterior." He winked at me.

I felt myself flushing. "Did you folks see George? I want to apologize again. He took the day off and left before I could say anything."

"We know. I am almost finished with work, and the plan is to go straight to his place, make sure he isn't moping. Thibault is covering for Charlene, so he finishes late but will join us after. Do you have any actual suspects, or is it still all up in the air?" Sam said.

"Not really. We have someone in custody, a man named Jason. We arrested him on suspicion of poaching. Probably nothing to do with our case, but at least that's one more lead to follow."

Marcus clapped me on the shoulder, holding two to-go cups and a small bag that smelled delicious from here. To get rid of the calories accumulated this week, I needed to work out some tonight.

"Let's go back and see what we can figure out from all of this."

We walked to the station, debating the best approach.

Once there, Mary told us the analysis on the knife and the piece found at the duck pond matched. It was a piece of antler from the handle of the knife. It must have been broken during the fight.

We spent the afternoon trying to make Jason talk, but his lawyer made sure he didn't say anything incriminating. Not even for the poaching.

Around six, we took a break to check our emails. We hadn't heard from the app company earlier, so I was happily surprised to find they had a name for us.

What we read on the screen made my blood run cold. "Shit," Marcus barked.

"We need someone to go to his house. Let's go to the garage. We might find him there."

My phone rang. When I saw Thibault's name on the display, I hesitated. I didn't want my head chewed off for what I'd done to George.

I still thank my lucky star to this day that Marcus decided for me.

He pressed the green button and put it on speaker. "Hey, Thibault. How are you doing? No dead body this time, right?" he joked. We both blanched when we heard a voice that wasn't Thibault's on the phone. I grabbed my phone and ran

for Mary. Behind me, Marcus was on his phone calling reinforcements.

"Mary, hit record on my phone. We will be on the radio at
the library."

And just as we had done a little over a week ago, we both
rushed right out of the door toward the library.

## 19

## Still Saturday

*E*arly evening on Saturday, I was ready to close. I couldn't wait to go see George. Poor man. He needed us to be there for him. I hadn't heard or seen Jack since Thursday until this morning, and what he had done to George didn't sit well with me. Yes, it was his job, but there were other ways to handle things, weren't there?

I was happy this week was done and couldn't wait to relax tomorrow. I debated sending a text to Jack so we could talk. Maybe a nice cold late lunch. The heat was getting to me. I was used to a humid climate, but my life in Ireland had not prepared me for seventy-three degrees in April. They were announcing some rain for next week, and I had all my fingers crossed it would happen. I loved the smell, my plants would be happy, and the drop in temperature would be more than welcome.

Sitting at my little table away from the front desk, I took

my phone out, already wording a text to Jack in my head. I heard footsteps behind me and called out, "I am sorry. We are closed." Whoever it was must have entered through the employee door. I had been at the book stack, sorting it so placing them back on the right shelves would be faster. Then I'd closed the front door before sitting to prepare my to-do list for the next day. Unless the police department had a key, no one would be able to come in without making a noise or being seen.

Then I heard a click. I'd watched enough crime movies and TV series to know how a gun sounded. I would have preferred to stay ignorant about how right they were. Hoping whoever was behind me hadn't noticed my phone, as I had it low on my lap, I quickly opened my contacts and pressed Call on the one man I hoped could help me. I lowered the sound as much as I could, locked the screen and, as I stood, dropped my phone in my back pocket.

The person I found facing me with a gun was definitely unexpected. Not that you could ever really expect someone to hold you at gunpoint, could you? Well, unless you were in law enforcement, but even to them, it must come as a nasty surprise.

Tom stood a short way from the desk in full view of the door. I was so screwed.

We stared at each other, unsure of what came next. He seemed frozen in place, but his hand was steady and the gun pointed at my head. Who knows what went over me? I was panicking inside, chanting a mix of "Oh, mon Dieu," "Merde," and "Really?" Out loud, in a very calm voice, looking him straight in the eye, I said, "I am sorry, Tom. Like I said, we are closed. Why don't you come back on Monday? Unless you know already which book you need. I can pick it up for you."

"Hi, Thibault. I am sorry to barge in, but we have to leave now."

Huh. Not exactly how I thought this was going to go.

"I am sorry, Tom, but I am not going anywhere. It's closing time, and I need to go visit George."

He took a step forward, then another. I tried to back away, but there wasn't much space between the table and the front desk. "Tom, what are you doing?"

"We need to go. Now. Before they find me. I can't, Thibault. It was a mistake. But you can help me make it better. Can't you?"

I was leaning against the counter and couldn't really go anywhere else. I was trapped. Cold sweat ran down my back. My heart pounded so hard it was all I could hear. "What did you do? What happened, Tom? Why don't we talk about it?"

"Talk? There is no time to talk, Thibault."

"Let's make time. Please. Please tell me what happened? What's wrong?"

"Everything's wrong. Why did you have to do this?"

"What did I do? I just need to know. So I can apologize or help you make it better." I swallowed. This made less and less sense.

"Why do you have to be so nice? Couldn't you be an asshole like everyone else? Reject me and be done with it? Why did you stop answering me but kept asking me for drinks as 'friends'? Playing hot and cold all this time."

Now I was confused on top of scared and angry. What the hell was going on? I didn't play games. And what messages? "What messages, Tom? I always answer your texts. Maybe not straightaway if I am busy at work, but otherwise, I always answer as quickly as I can."

"Not those. The ones on the app. You ghosted me. Was it

simply because I got scared to meet you? Isn't that a little mean? You could have given me a second chance. But no. You had to hook up with him," he spat.

"I am not sure I understand. I deleted all the dating apps I had almost two years ago. A couple of men harassed me. To top it off, the ones propositioning me were all looking for a 'boy,' and I am anything but. Are you the sweet man who never showed for our date? I sent him a message I wouldn't be on there anymore, but he never answered, and I deleted my account. Was it you?"

"Yes. But I didn't think you meant it. When I didn't receive answers, I thought you might respond better to my letters, but you never mentioned them."

"I am sorry, Tom. I didn't know they were from you. Some were very sweet."

The gun was lower now but still pointed at me. I tried to edge around the desk, but Tom stopped me. "Where do you think you are going?"

"Nowhere. I just wanted to find a comfortable spot to sit so we could talk. It looks like this is all a big misunderstanding. Why won't you tell me what's wrong? Why are you here tonight, Tom? You could have sent me a text. I would have joined you for a drink at the Tavern."

"No, you wouldn't," he sneered. "You probably have another hot date with your new toy, don't you? Is that why you are trying to run away from me? Well, you are not going anywhere. Especially not running to him. I won't let you. You are mine. I killed a woman for you. You are not going anywhere!" His last words were shouted in my face.

I crumpled right where Sally Anne had been posed. By Tom. Oh god.

"You were the one sending me the letters? Why did you kill her, Tom?"

"She was always on your case. I didn't want to, but she didn't leave me a choice!" he shouted. "She didn't listen when I tried to talk some sense into her. She blocked me. When I saw her, I knew I had to make sure she got the message. And then she was dead. It happened so fast. I am so sorry." His voice dropped to a whisper.

This didn't make any sense.

"So now you understand. We need to go. They will take you away from me, and I can't live with that. We can run. I know places where they won't find us. We can be happy. I'll buy you all the books you want. We can have animals, a family, love. All we have ever dreamed of. But we need to go now."

He grabbed my arm, pulling me up and trying to drag me. I made myself as heavy as I could, but he was so much stronger. "Wait, wait! Tom. Please wait. Why don't we leave a note? Explain what happened. It was an accident, wasn't it? I know you—you wouldn't hurt someone deliberately, would you? Why don't you tell me, and I can write it down? Let them know so they won't look for us."

He stopped, contemplating what I'd said. I tried to take a step back, but his hold on me tightened, and I bit back a pained cry.

"Hmm. That makes sense. There." He pulled me to the other side of the desk and sat me on the chair. He grabbed a pen and paper and continued. "You can write. Tell them it wasn't my fault. She wouldn't quit hurting you. I had to make her stop."

I took the pen and looked back at Tom. "Can you tell me what happened?" I hoped Jack was listening. That Jason guy was innocent after all, at least of murdering Sally Anne. Unless... "Did Jason help you? Is that why you think they are coming for you? You're afraid he will talk?"

His face was drawn with fear, then anger. With a scowl, he said, "It was his fault. If he hadn't been there, she would still be alive."

"Did he kill Sally Anne? If you only helped him move her..."

He interrupted me. "That man isn't capable of killing anyone. Only poor creatures that never asked for it," he spat. "I knew where she walked her dog every night, past my house. After her last accusations against you, I knew I had to do something before she ran you off or made you straight or something."

Not how it would have gone, but sure.

He kept talking. "I followed her and put on a scarf so she wouldn't see my face. When I saw no one else was around, I knew it was the perfect time. I walked to her and told her to leave you alone. She started screeching at me. About perversion, how men like us are predators and shouldn't be left around young children. That you were corrupting the youth in this town. I told her to stop screaming. That nobody cared. That you were a good man. Jason came around the corner, covered in blood and holding a knife. She started screaming. Tried to run away. Jason grabbed her. He dropped his knife, and I grabbed it. Sally Anne escaped his hold somehow. She was still screaming. Her dog was barking and trying to attack Jason.

"She ran straight at me and tried to grab the knife. I don't know why she didn't just run. We struggled, and the knife caught her throat. I didn't mean to.

"She fell. We tried to stop the bleeding, but there was so much blood. Jason grabbed the leash of the dog and tied him to a bench. He told me to pick up Sally Anne, and we placed her in the trunk of his car. He told me it was too early. Someone would see us if we tried to dump the body. He grabbed the dog and walked me back to my house. I told him we should call the police, but he said they wouldn't believe us. When he asked where we could hide the body, I told him the library. It wouldn't be hidden long, but I thought it would prove I was worthy of you."

He stopped then, seeming to calm down as he recounted the events leading to Sally Anne's death. For all her faults, she hadn't deserved anything so awful. Dorothy was right. Though my hand was not the one that gave the fatal blow, I was responsible for Sally Anne's death. If I had just let her talk and never fought back, she might have stopped a long time ago, and she would still be alive.

Tom started talking again, angrier than I had ever seen him. "But instead of being happy and thankful for my little present, you ran straight into his arms. He never gave you the time of day, even after your hookup, but it didn't stop you falling for his pretty face and his lies. Forgetting everything around you and never saying thank you to me. You should have fallen into my arms. Answered my letters. Come to me for comfort. But nooo."

He waved the gun in my face. "Write. Now. And then we go. I will teach you to love me and show you how to be thankful for everything I do for you."

I wrote. I am not sure what. Words fell on the page. As soon as I finished, Tom grabbed me. I caught something then, a glint from the corridor. Someone was there. Scrambling for time, I said, "Why don't you read what I wrote? I just want to make sure I did it right."

He bent over the desk to read, giving time for Jack and Marcus to slowly walk into the room. I almost crumpled in relief.

Tom looked at me. "What is this?" He waved the paper in

my face. "You didn't write it was an accident. What are you playing at?"

"I am sorry. This is a lot to take in, Tom. I can rewrite it. Make it better."

A sound that didn't come from either of us echoed through the room. I froze and Tom turned, grabbing me once again by the arm. Jack and Marcus had their guns drawn, closer than I'd thought.

**Jack**

We arrived at the library at the same time as John. I told him to take point at the front door. It would most likely be closed. From what both Thibault and Charlene told me, they closed it first thing in the evenings. It opened to the inside, so John could kick it in if we needed him in a hurry. Thankfully, the shutters weren't down yet. The back door was open, which was good. I wasn't sure if Tom had used Sally Anne's key or if the last person to leave had forgotten to close it, but it didn't matter. It allowed us to get in with minimal noise. We switched off our radios so no sound could alert Tom to our presence.

Once we were in the corridor, all we could hear was Tom and Thibault anyway. We slowly and carefully moved forward. Tom was still speaking with Thibault. Then shuffling. He must have pushed Thibault to the desk. My heart was beating in my ears, and I could barely hear anything else. God, now I understood why it was hard for people to date law enforcement officers or anyone who had to deal with violence. Not that Thibault fell in either category, but being here to rescue him brought forward feelings of anxiety I had never experienced before, especially for someone else.

When we reached the end of the corridor, Marcus slowly put his head out and made a motion with his hand for us to switch places. I looked, careful not to move too far. The way they were positioned meant that, for the time being, Tom's back was to us. John was not visible at the front doors, but I knew he was in place.

Thibault must have noticed us because he distracted Tom by asking him to look at the letter he had written. While Tom was bent over the desk, I signaled for Marcus to follow me, and we went in, keeping low and taking cover behind tables. We probably looked ridiculous, but we needed to be as invisible as possible. If he shot at Thibault, we could do nothing, but we would have the right angle to take him down. And if he heard us and shot in our direction, we had a bit of cover. At that moment, the top of my wish list was his being a lousy shot. I hadn't even known he possessed a gun, which meant it was either illegal or he had gotten it from Jason.

They were both at the desk looking down. Marcus moved forward, and his arm caught on the back of a chair. The sound echoed in the empty library. We both froze.

Tom turned toward us. Our number was up. We both stood, guns pointed straight at his chest.

It could have been utter chaos. He could have shot and taken us all out. Or ducked and hidden. Or used Thibault as a shield. But he stood there, frozen, holding Thibault's right arm and the gun in his left hand. I couldn't remember if he was right- or left-handed. Not that it mattered too much. One wrong move and someone could get hurt or worse. But if we were lucky and it was his weak arm, it would give us an advantage.

He whirled toward Thibault and shouted, "You called him?

Why the hell would you do that? It was going so well. We were supposed to escape. They weren't supposed to find us. What did you do?"

"I am sorry. I didn't mean to. You scared me," Thibault cried.

"Hey, Tom. Why don't you drop the gun? I am sure there is a simple explanation here. Why don't you just talk to us?" Marcus said.

"Why, so you can shoot me? You lower your guns first." He let go of Thibault's arm and came forward. "If you want him, you will have to go through me. No one can separate us. We are in love, and we are leaving."

He turned around, reaching for Thibault again, but Thibault went around the desk and edged toward the doors. "Where are you going? Are you choosing him again? Over me? After everything we just said?"

Thibault pleaded. "Tom. I am sorry. I don't know what to do. I don't want them to hurt us. Why don't you listen and lower your gun? It will be okay, I promise."

The fear on Thibault's face made my heart hurt. I wanted to rush to him and protect him. Marcus sensing that whispered, "Jack, don't," before saying to Tom in a clearer voice, "Tom, it's all right. We only want to talk. Here, we will lower our guns. Why don't you do the same?"

We both did, slowly, ready to bring them back up at any sign Tom would shoot.

Tom glared at us, then looked back at Thibault. "I won't let him take you away from me."

Marcus shouted, "Tom. Don't!"

Tom pulled the trigger at the same time I did. Two cries of pain rang out, and Tom's gun flew off in a wild arc. John came through the front door at the same time Marcus pushed Tom to the floor, and I ran to the gun and Thibault.

After that, it was utter chaos. The EMTs Mary had radioed had waited with John at the front entrance, hidden to the side. One paramedic took care of Tom, while the other worked on Thibault. When Tom was put on the stretcher, we handcuffed him to it, and Marcus left with the ambulance. By the time we were done, Thibault was gone.

## 20

JACK

**Saturday – Late Night**

*T*onight was one of the worst of my life. I hadn't expected things to go the way they did, and I couldn't help thinking we'd missed something that would have prevented it from happening.

My bullet went through Tom's shoulder, doing no damage to the bones or anything else, and he had only needed stitches. They wanted to keep him at the hospital for a couple of days. Once released, he would make his way to the county jail. He wasn't talking, but with his confession on tape, I hoped Jason would talk in the morning.

I went to the hospital to check with Marcus and make sure someone would guard Tom's room. As soon as I was done, I went up to Thibault's room. The bullet had gone in the meaty part of his right arm; he'd had stitches as well, and they would release him in the morning. Or so the nurse told me. I hadn't seen Thibault yet.

Instead, I was sitting in a visitor's chair in the lobby, not far from his room. I didn't know what to say. Guilt kept running through me. At first, I'd focused all of my energy on making sure Thibault hadn't committed the crime. Once his name was cleared, I should have pushed the judge and the companies to get an answer sooner. We might not have caught Jason, but we could have arrested Tom more quickly.

I rubbed my hands on my jeans, stood, and went to knock on Thibault's door. A soft "Enter" came from within, and I walked in. He looked small and so pale, almost the color of his sheets. I walked toward him. Careful to not hurt his shoulder further, I bent down and hugged him on the left side.

"I am so sorry, sweetheart. This shouldn't have happened. We missed something. It all went so fast. You can't know how sorry I am for everything that went down. I should have protected you better."

I rested my head in the crook of his neck, inhaling his scent. It was very faint, drowned by the smells of the hospital and antiseptic, but here, so close to his skin, I caught a hint of lavender. I kissed the warm skin of his neck. I moved back a little, and he caught my lips with his. He must have moved wrong, as he hissed in pain.

I moved back and grabbed the visitor's chair to sit down. He stayed quiet, eyeing me. "It wasn't your fault, Jack. It was mine. I should have reported the letters much earlier. Apparently, Tom kept sending me messages and only started sending me mail because I didn't answer him anymore. If I had reported it or stopped answering Sally Anne when she was antagonizing me, we wouldn't be here. I am sorry."

"What? No. None of this was your fault. Tom killed Sally Anne, not you. You had nothing to do with any of this. Don't you dare think that."

He kept shaking his head, and a tear fell down his face. I

took his left hand in both of mine and squeezed. He tried to take his hand away, but I held fast.

His watery chuckle mended and broke my heart at the same time. My poor Thibault. This should never have happened to him. He tried to pull his hand again and mock-growled. "Silly man. I like it when you hold my hand, but I can't move my right one, so how am I going to wipe the tears off my face?"

Pleased at his admission, I smiled and wiped the tears off his face myself. "There. Done. Now promise me you will remove any thoughts of you being guilty from your mind. Please."

He went to shrug and grimaced when it pulled at his right shoulder. "I can't stop thinking about that, Jack. If it wasn't for me, Sally Anne would still be alive. It keeps running through my head."

"We need to shut your brain out then, don't we?" Leaning forward, I kissed him carefully so we wouldn't jostle his shoulder.

We heard a throat clearing, and I moved back. A nurse was standing at the door, fists on her hips. "Now Detective, I thought you wanted to question him. If you are here for a more personal reason, I am going to ask you to leave. My patient needs rest if he wants to leave in the morning."

I gave Thibault a brief peck on the lips and stood. "I will come and see you in the morning before you leave if I can."

He nodded and winced again. Sheepishly, he smiled at me. "Thank you. For everything tonight. I will see you tomorrow."

The nurse ushered me out.

&a.

On Sunday, I woke up feeling far from refreshed. I'd had no trouble falling asleep, but the sleeping itself had been even more difficult. It had been riddled by nightmares of a dying Thibault, mixed in with Ruth telling me she'd thought better of me. And of Helene, Thibault's mom, asking why I had let her bébé be taken away from her.

All in all, not restful.

When I arrived at the hospital later that day, a different nurse was at the station, and she told me a doctor would check on Thibault shortly. I went to his room and heard distinct voices. I didn't want to intrude, so I retreated. I wasn't sure what we were to each other and didn't want to have that conversation in front of his parents or friends. And I couldn't pretend to be there on police business.

Before I could make my escape, a voice I hadn't heard in too long called out my name. No, not my name—Ruth's nickname for me, Jacko. I stopped dead in my tracks.

Helene's hand squeezed my shoulder before she moved in front of me. She lifted on her toes, small thing that she was, kissed my cheek and whispered, "Thank you." I broke down then and cried. I couldn't fathom why she would thank me when I hadn't been able to protect her son. To say nothing of the way I had been around him for the past two years, going so far as trying to convince myself he was guilty of murder.

"For what?" I asked in a broken voice.

She held me for a few minutes before leading me to a row of plastic chairs. "Dear boy, don't be silly. For saving my Thibault last night."

"No, I didn't," I interrupted hoarsely.

She handed me a tissue and continued. "Ah, ces hommes. Don't tell me I am wrong. Thibault himself is very thankful you came in when you did. He said without you gentlemen, he would have died."

"We should have seen it earlier, done something sooner. This was not supposed to happen, Helene. I should have protected him."

"Shush, mon lapin. You are fine. You saved my baby, and that's what matters. And I wanted to say merci. So just take it, all right?" Somewhat reluctantly, I nodded, but I knew she wouldn't let it go. This was one stubborn woman.

"I didn't want to disturb you guys. How is he this morning? Are you guys staying with him for a few days?"

She smiled and patted my arm. "Why don't you come over and have a look for yourself, Jacko?"

My phone vibrated. I pulled it out and read a text from Marcus.

*With Tom. Come when you can? He is not talking to me, but might answer to you.*

"I can't right now. I have to go to work. I was just stopping by on my way up."

"Oh. Pity. Well, why don't you come over later at Thibault's home and have some food with us?"

"I'll try." I smiled. "But no promises. It will probably take us a while to sort through everything."

She shook her head. "Don't get lost in your work, Jack. Thibault will be happy to see you, I am sure. You can bring Marcus with you so we can thank him properly as well."

"Will do, Helene."

I stood and gave her another hug, which by the look of surprise and happiness on her face, she hadn't expected. Neither had I, but it felt too nice to pass up.

"I have to go. I'll see you later."

I was going to turn and leave when I noticed Thibault leaning against the doorjamb and took one step toward him. He had a frown on his face, looking from me to his mother. "You met before?" he asked.

Looking embarrassed, his mom moved toward him. "Oui. There might be some things we need to talk about."

"You think? Maman! You never said anything. About Ruth or Jack. What the hell?"

I made to move toward him, but he waved me off. "I'll see you later, Jack. My mother and I need to discuss some things." Smiling, he turned around and winked. "I do expect you at my house, though. Don't think either of us will forget. And do bring Marcus."

I waved back and left, taking the stairs to the unit above. Since they'd both suffered similar wounds, Tom and Thibault should have been on the same floor. But they moved Tom to the psych ward, as the doctors thought he was having the beginning of a psychotic break. They sedated him last night. I wondered if that was why he wouldn't talk to Marcus.

Marcus was standing outside his room. "How you doing, man? I got your text. I was talking to Thibault's mom."

"How is he doing?" Marcus asked, a frown of concern on his face.

"He looked better this morning. They want us to go eat with them later. I told them no promises, as I have the feeling it will take a while to wade through all this."

Marcus smiled. "I am glad to hear it. The doctors just came for Tom. They should release him tomorrow. He is not talking, at least to me. I am hoping seeing you might make him. Especially if you bring news of Thibault."

"All right, let's go in, then."

We softly knocked on the door and walked inside. On his hospital bed, Tom looked pale and tired. His left hand was cuffed to the bed.

We both took a seat on the visitor's chairs. "Hey, Tom. Marcus talked to your doctors. You should have a full recovery, they said, and we should be able to move you tomorrow."

He looked vacant, and his face stayed blank at my words.

"I saw Thibault just now. He looks okay. He should recover as well. Like you, it was only a flesh wound to the right shoulder. Why did you shoot Thibault, Tom?"

"I want to see him," he whispered, his face unchanged. No emotions showed at all.

"Tom, you know we can't do that. But I need to know what happened. Maybe we can still help you."

"Help me?" he mocked. "So you can swoop in and be the big hero?" He laughed, but there was no joy to it. A scowl on his face, he looked at me then. "He is mine. You will never have him. It was all an accident. You have no proof against me. I will get out, and I'll show him how good we could be together. He will forget all about you." He paused, eyes wild. "This is all your fault. You hurt my Thibault. All your fault!" he shouted.

His monitor started going wild, and nurses rushed in. They pushed us out. His doctor said he didn't recommend us seeing him anymore. They would contact the psychiatric facility for the criminally insane.

We left for the precinct then. We wouldn't be getting anything from Tom.

Jason was brought back into the interrogation room. We played the tape of last night's conversation between Thibault and Tom.

Jason's lawyer looked defeated and told him to give us as many details as he could. Jason's story agreed with Tom's.

Marcus interrupted him after he explained how Sally Anne had died. "Why didn't you call emergency services? Say it was an accident."

"If she wasn't really dead, she would accuse us of attempted murder. And I had just killed a buck. I knew how that would look. People wouldn't think Tom did it. The fault would fall on me. And I love Tom like a brother but not enough to take the fall for him."

"How did you end up bringing her to the library?" I asked.

"When we got back to Tom's, we cleaned ourselves. At first, Tom kept repeating, 'Oh my god.' After we washed up, a sense of calm fell on him, and he started talking to himself. Things like, 'It would be such a delightful surprise. A wonderful present. Maybe he will understand it's from me, and finally we can be together.'"

"Why did you follow his idea of bringing her to the library?"

"I guess the shock of everything had set in by then, and I didn't really think about what we were doing. Just following Tom's lead. He looked so cool and collected. Like he knew how to handle things. I didn't question it."

"Why did you stay? Why not go back to Oklahoma or somewhere else?"

"I don't know. I was scared Tom would lose it. In the end, the little dog cost us everything. I took him with us when we went back to Tom's. I took care of him, but yesterday morning he escaped. I tried looking for him and thought maybe he went back to the duck pond. So I went there. And then further. I don't know why I took my rifle with me. It's not like I intended to shoot or anything. Habit, I guess."

That dog deserved a treat for sure.

After that, we wrapped up. We went back to our desks and worked on the case file, making sure it was airtight and ready for the prosecutor. The chief came around to thank us for a job well done. I couldn't help the guilt rising in me again. All I could see was Thibault's terror and the sound of the gun.

Marcus looked as exhausted as I felt. We called it a night. After a quick dinner, I fell into bed. I woke up the next day to a couple of messages from Thibault inviting me over. I texted back saying I would come over after work.

The library was closed for the day, so we made sure we had photographic evidence of where everyone had been during the shooting. We picked up Thibault's letter on the desk. There wasn't much to it. More jumbled thoughts and "Sorry" here and there.

Marcus went with me to see Thibault. I was hoping he could distract Thibault's parents while we talked.

It didn't go according to plan.

Helene ushered us inside and introduced us to her husband, Henri. Every time Helene had seen Ruth, she had been alone. Ruth told me it was because they enjoyed gossiping, and ladies didn't like men to eavesdrop on that. I had laughed but understood. Some things you would never say in front of your husband or wife.

Herding us to the kitchen, she made us sit and called for Thibault. He came shuffling in, his hair a mess, his pajama pants in slight disarray, and he had only one sleeve pulled through on his T-shirt.

She clucked at him and made him sit. He took the seat right next to me, and we smiled at each other. When his hand brushed mine, I grabbed for it. As it was his right, I was gentle but happy to know he wouldn't be able to use it, which meant I could keep hold of it. Taking in the table in front of me, I blushed at the reminder of the things we'd done here what felt like a lifetime ago.

"Can I get either of you something to drink?" Helene asked swiftly, her French accent coming through. "Any tea, or do you prefer coffee?"

"Tea," we both said at the same time, and Marcus shot me a grin. She took out a pitcher of sweet tea from the fridge and poured us all a glass. Marcus's grin widened when she put a plate of cookies in front of us.

"You shouldn't have. But thank you," I said, picking one, while Marcus mumbled a quick "Thanks" between two bites.

Helene sat. "Thibault, why don't you tell your friends the good news?"

He frowned at her, shaking his head. When he saw us all looking at him, he sighed. "I am leaving on an extended vacation. First, I'll stay with my parents for a few days, and then I'll see. I'd like to visit my sister and her wife and maybe go see one of my old college friends."

"You're leaving?" I asked. "Why?"

Sensing a sudden tension in the room, Helene grabbed Marcus and Henri, and they all went outside.

"I can't work. The doctor has put me on mandatory rest and then rehab for the next month, maybe a month and a half. My mother is threatening to stay to take care of me. And I love my mam dearly, but I can't be babied for a month. She will drive me crazy. So the compromise was to stay with my parents for a week and then go from there."

"You could stay with me. Or I could stay with you."

"Don't be silly, Jack. We barely know each other. We are not even friends. What happens if after a day or two, we already get on each other's nerves? I will be back to square one. I think it would do me some good. All I can think of is Sally Anne, Tom, and getting shot in the library. I am not going forever, just a few weeks."

Deep down, I knew he was right. It was his health, mental and physical, after all, but I couldn't help the feeling he was running away from me and he might not come back. "I have the name and number of a very good psychotherapist who works with our police department, if you want to contact him?"

"Thank you. I have one from the hospital, but it's good to keep my options open."

I gave him the card. I didn't know what else to say. "You know it wasn't your fault? What happened to Sally Anne or to you?"

"I know, I guess. Though I can't stop thinking it was."

We both fell silent. I looked at him and couldn't help kissing him. "Something for you to remember and make you come back here."

We looked at each other. I would have kissed him some more, but I heard Marcus's voice close by, which stopped me.

We left shortly after that. Whatever happened next, I really hoped Thibault would come back.

# EPILOGUE

**Thibault**

Just as I was about to go, it finally started raining. George and Sam had helped me pack my things the night before.

In my absence, Steve would come take care of the animals. George and Sam both said they would try and visit every couple of days to stay inside, water my plants, and keep the cats and dogs company. They offered to Skype or WhatsApp so the animals wouldn't think I had abandoned them.

After my parents left on Tuesday, I thought I might be okay. But that night, the nightmares started again, more violent than before. I could do things with my left arm, but it proved more difficult than I'd anticipated. I'd tried to go to the library yesterday but hadn't been able to go farther than the door. Between the look on people's faces and remembering what had happened at the front desk, I'd had a panic attack. George, who had taken the day off to help me around, rushed me out to a bench in the park. When we tried to go to the

Miracle Brew, the number of people trying to ask me questions was too much.

I had contacted the therapist already, and I had a good feeling about him. When I told him about my experience at the library and my idea of going away, he encouraged it. He did phone sessions and said fitting me in wouldn't be a problem.

I surveyed the house one last time. As I made my way to the front, a car door slammed.

I opened the front door, ready to leave. My bags were already in the car, so I could talk to whoever it was outside. Closing the door, I walked toward the car.

Jack came closer, and I stopped.

"I wanted to come today to try and stop you from leaving. Maybe be a bit melodramatic, to guilt you into staying with me. But I heard what happened yesterday, and I understand. I am not happy about you leaving, and I really hope you meant it when you said you would come back."

I walked to him, stood on my tiptoes, and whispered in his ear, "You can count on it."

I gave him a soft, lingering kiss, then stepped away and walked to my car without looking back. If I had, I wouldn't have gone, and that wasn't the right thing for me right now.


The End - Until next time

# AFTERWORD

Thank you for reading this book. As you might know, reviews are the bread and butter of authors. If you enjoyed this book, please consider leaving a review.

What's next in the Weatherboro mystery series is book 2.

There we will meet again with all these wonderful people and some new characters. The title should be 'Antiques and relationships'.

If you would like more details, please follow me on social media or subscribe to my newsletter.

# ACKNOWLEDGMENTS

I want to say a big thank you to the people who have helped me through this journey.

First David, my critic partner on this book who gave me great advice.

Megan, my beta reader, for all her help on making this book what it is today. The plot was confused but thanks to her it came out great.

M.A. who did a great job as my editor. It was my first time and I really appreciated the help, time and effort she put into it.

Jennifer for a great job at correcting all my mistakes, big and small.

My boyfriend, my mom, family and friends for their support and encouragements.

And lastly, you, the readers for taking a chance on me. Hope you enjoyed reading this book as much as I loved writing it and that you will enjoy what's coming next.

Thank you.

# ABOUT THE AUTHOR

CP FRAISE is a very French person who has been haunting the East coast of Ireland for the past thirteen years. She enjoys a quiet life there with her boyfriend and two cats.

She fell in love with romance when she was ten and stumbled upon her grandma's collection. She started reading MM romance a few years ago and never looked back.

Food, animals and love are the main ingredients she loves in books and life.

You can connect with CP Fraise through her website cpfraiseauthor.com (and subscribe to her newsletter there) or use the links below

facebook.com/cp.fraise.author

instagram.com/cp.fraise.author

goodreads.com/cp_fraise_author